SPLINTERED ICE

WYNCOTE WOLVES

BOOK SIX

CALI MELLE

*For the ones who can see past the grey clouds in the sky...
there's always sunshine on the other side*

PROLOGUE
STERLING

"Yo, Barrett," Simon calls after me as we head out of the locker room following practice. It's our first practice back together after winter break. A brand-new semester and we're gearing up for the most important games of our college career. "You wanna go grab some beers?"

Simon has been my roommate since junior year. We shared our house with Hayden when he first moved here, but since he and Eden became exclusive, he moved out. Simon and I decided to let Vaughn Carter move in with us. He's a freshman at Wyncote this year, but he is practically a goddamn prodigy.

The kid is destined for greatness and there are

talks of him going pro before graduating college. I wish I were going to be around to see how things pan out for him, but the rest of us are all going to be graduating this year.

"Hell yeah," I tell him, nodding enthusiastically. "I'll meet you at O'Hallarans?"

"Sounds good," Simon agrees as he heads through the parking lot in the direction of his car. Sometimes we drive together to save on gas, but he had to run some errands after class so I didn't bother questioning him.

After throwing my hockey equipment into the trunk, I hop into the front seat of my car. As I turn on the engine, my phone connects to the car and it begins to ring. Glancing at the screen, a groan slips from my lips as I see my little sister's name flashing across it.

"What's up, Stella?" I answer, attempting to keep the irritation from my voice. She's three years younger than me and decided to move across the country to attend college. It pissed my parents off, but I was secretly thankful. Don't get me wrong, I love my little sister and will protect her with my life... but goddamn if she doesn't get on my nerves sometimes.

When I spoke to her two days ago, she was

trying to get me to send her some money to go out since our parents wouldn't. They want her to get a job, since they're paying for her schooling. Being the brother that I am, I sent her some, but it feels like she only calls me when she needs something now.

"Hey, big brother!" Her voice is energetic and she sounds like she's bouncing off the walls. I know she's been partying and shit, but sometimes I wonder what she's really getting herself into. "Is now a bad time?"

"Nope, just finished practice and I'm heading to the bar."

"Okay, cool," she says, pausing for a moment. "So, I have a huge favor to ask of you."

Internally, I groan, closing my eyes for a second before pulling out onto the road. "What is it?" God knows what the hell she's going to be asking of me now.

"So... Olivia just transferred to Wyncote this semester."

My eyebrows pull together as I drive closer to the bar. "Olivia? Like your best friend since kindergarten?"

"Yes, stupid," Stella scoffs, and I swear I can hear her rolling her eyes. "As if there is any other Olivia who practically lived at our house."

My mind instantly drifts back to Olivia Davis. I haven't seen her since I left for college. She was only fifteen at the time, still practically a child. She always wanted to be treated like she was older, but I couldn't bring myself to view her as anyone other than my little sister's best friend. I literally could not allow myself to look at her any other way.

"Why's she coming to Wyncote?"

"Well, she's majoring in biology. For some reason, Wyncote is supposed to have a better program for whatever it is she's doing." Stella pauses for a moment and I hear someone talking in the background but she shushes them. "I honestly don't remember why she said it was better there. Either way, she's there... like now."

"And this affects me, how?"

Stella sighs. "Can you not be an asshole for, like, two seconds?"

"Can you maybe call me sometime when you don't need something from me?"

Stella laughs. "Don't act like you would actually want to talk to me. Unless it has to do with hockey, you tend to tune everyone out."

My jaw tightens, but I don't bother arguing with her. As I pull my car into a spot in the parking lot at O'Hallarans, I see Simon as he walks inside.

"Get to the point, Stella. I need to get off the phone."

"Olivia just moved there and doesn't know a single person. Can you do me a favor and just, like, check up on her? Maybe make sure she's okay and keep an eye out on her?"

"Don't you think she's old enough to take care of herself?" I question my sister as I turn off the engine of my car and switch the call back to my phone. Climbing out of the car, I hold it to my ear before slamming the door shut behind me.

Stella groans through the phone and I can tell she's getting frustrated with me. It's only natural; it's the relationship we have together. There was a point where we got along really well, until we both started to grow up and grow apart. I will always look out for her, but we are definitely in two different places in our lives right now.

"Please, Sterling," Stella practically begs. "You know I wouldn't ask something like this from you if it wasn't important to me."

A sigh slips from my lips as I make my way closer to the entrance of the bar. "Fine," I agree, not entirely pleased about the entire situation. "How the hell do you expect me to find her? I'm not going to go search the dorms looking for her. Do you know where she's living or anything about her being here."

"Look," my sister says, her words rushing out. "I'm gonna text you her number, and just shoot her a message. Meet up with her and shit. I don't know, just let me know as soon as you do."

"What? No. I'm not going to do—"

"Thanks, Sterling!" Stella is rushing me off the phone now and her tone is filled with excitement. "I knew I could count on my big brother. You're seriously the best. Sending her number now, love you!"

Stella ends the call before I even get the chance to say anything to her in response. She completely set me up. I agreed to check in on her friend and keep an eye out on her, but I didn't need her damn number. If Stella could have just given me some information about her, I could have figured it out without having to meet up with her.

A text comes through from Stella with Olivia's number and a reminder to send her a message ASAP and then to let Stella know. Groaning, I save the number in my phone and open my messages. I stare at the screen for a moment as I linger outside the door of O'Hallarans, not knowing what the fuck to say.

STERLING

Hey, is this Olivia? This is Sterling, Stella's brother.

I cringe, rereading my message. What the hell was that? The stupidest thing I've ever sent. Sighing, I lock my phone and put it into the front pocket of my hoodie before heading into the bar.

Simon is already sitting there waiting for me. He turns to face me, handing me a beer that he already ordered for me as I drop down onto the barstool next to him. "I talked to Greyson. He's heading over here too."

"Cool," I respond, nodding as I lift the beer to my lips and take a sip. My phone vibrates in my front pocket and I pull it out. I see Olivia's name on the screen and exhale deeply.

"Who's Olivia?" Simon questions me, his nosey ass looking over my shoulder at my phone.

Turning my head to him, I narrow my eyes, my lips pursed. "My little sister's best friend. She just moved here and Stella wanted me to check in on her."

"Ooh," Simon raises his eyebrows, "is she hot?"

I drive my shoulder into his, pushing him away. "Fuck off and don't even think about it."

Simon chuckles, turning his direction back to

the TV at the hockey replays as I open Olivia's message. My jaw tics as my eyes scan the screen.

OLIVIA

> Hi Sterling! How are you doing? I don't know if Stella told you, but I just moved to Wyncote.

She's just as fucking bubbly as I remember. And I hate it. That's how Olivia always was. The kindest, most caring person I had ever met. And she got under my skin like no other with the way positivity just rolled off her. She's like a ray of fucking sunshine and I would much rather see dark clouds lining the sky.

STERLING

> Stella did tell me. She wanted me to check in on you and make sure you were good.

Fuck what Stella wanted. I'm not meeting up with Olivia if I don't have to. If she doesn't need my help with anything, then there's no need.

OLIVIA

> I'm good! Just getting settled in and adjusting to life here :)

She would send a goddamn smiley face emoji. Grabbing my beer, I take another sip of it before sending my last response to her for the night.

STERLING

Cool. If you need anything, let me know.

I send a quick message to my sister, letting her know I talked to Olivia. Before either of them can respond, I put my phone on silent and lay it on the bar facedown. I'll do what my sister asked of me in terms of making sure Olivia is good.

We may have been close at one point, but that doesn't mean we were ever friends.

She's my sister's best friend, not mine.

CHAPTER ONE
OLIVIA

Making a move in the middle of my freshman year may have been a huge mistake. I did it because of my major and the program that Wyncote offered. It wasn't my first choice of schools because I wanted to go south. As soon as I was accepted to a university in Florida, that was it. I was finally getting out of the cold from living up north.

I should have put more consideration into which school would have been best for my forensic psychology degree, but I didn't. Life was something that I tried to live in a careful manner. I was never one who took risks, even though my best friend Stella was constantly living life on the edge. It about gave her family a heart attack with the way she behaved.

It was almost like I was a sounding board for her, someone safe who helped to keep her in line. That went out the window as soon as she decided she wanted to go to California for college. She had no idea what she was majoring in, but she wanted to get as far away from Vermont as I did.

It's funny how things work out, though, because here I am... back in the damn Arctic.

My first few days of class weren't as awkward as I imagined they would be. Thankfully, it was the start of a new semester, so it wasn't like I was coming in after classes already started. That's the nice thing about college. Even when making a move, there's not really such a thing as the new kid. I was able to find my place, even with being quiet and not really talking to anyone.

Moving into the dorms was probably the biggest challenge. Again, I was blessed with a roommate who seems relatively cool. I was a ball of anxiety before moving in here but as soon as I met Emery, I knew that it was for nothing. She doesn't seem like the partying type, but she spends a lot of time with her boyfriend, so I don't see her often. When I do, she's nothing but nice to me.

And then there was Sterling Barrett.

My best friend's older brother and the boy I crushed on for most of my high school years.

He was three years older than us and he's been at Wyncote the entire time. From what Stella has told me, he's made a place for himself on the hockey team.

And I know she was behind him texting me over the weekend.

It's literally been over three years since we last saw each other or talked. There's no reason why we would have talked after he left for college. We weren't exactly friends. I just so happened to be his little sister's best friend who practically lived at their house. Other than that, he was just the enigma that I watched from afar.

After he left, I got over my little crush on him. There was no point in wishing on a star that didn't exist. And in Sterling's eyes, I didn't exist. I had a boyfriend through high school, but we broke up the summer before college. It wasn't going anywhere and we were both going in separate directions in life.

Now that I'm back in Vermont, attending the same school as Sterling, I can't help it when my mind wanders to him. It's not a thought I let myself entertain, but it's one that tends to pop up every now and again.

When he reached out, he extended the open invitation to let him know if I needed anything, but I know Sterling. He didn't actually mean it. He's not the type who wants to be bothered by anyone. God forbid you ever get in his way.

As I walk through the hall after my last class, I adjust my backpack on my shoulders. Most of the other students are already filing out of the building, so I squeeze through a group that is hovering by the doorway. No one bothers to move out of the way, which seems to be pretty typical.

Walking down the steps from the front of the building, someone comes up behind me, bumping my shoulder as they rush past. It's a sudden moment of panic as I realize that I've reached the bottom of the stairs and there aren't any railings for me to grab onto as I lose my balance. I trip over my own feet, stumbling like a newborn calf in the most ungraceful manner possible.

Just as I'm about to go down, face-first onto the concrete, a pair of hands wrap around my biceps. I'm pulled back upright and I glance up, my eyes meeting Sterling's dark brown ones as he stares down at me. He holds me steady, until I regain my balance. His hands linger for a moment, my gaze searching his as he lingers in front of me.

"Thanks," I breathe, still a little shook up from the thought of almost eating shit in front of everyone. "Someone bumped into me and threw me off-balance."

"Yeah, I saw," Sterling replies with indifference. He runs his hand through his dark hair. It's longer than when I last saw him, the soft waves falling just below his eyebrows.

The air leaves my lungs in a rush as I'm practically starstruck by the sight of him. The past few years have been good to Sterling and it's clear that he's been working on his physique since he upped his hockey game. Back in high school, he was never scrawny, but he was caught in that awkward stage.

He's filled out since then and is taller than I remembered him being. Then again, the times that we were this close were few and far between. He's grown up, aging like a fine wine I wouldn't mind tasting.

What the hell is wrong with you, Liv?

"Are you good?" he questions me, his hands still lingering on my biceps. I drop my gaze to them, my heart pounding erratically in my chest. Sterling follows my gaze and quickly drops his hands away like I'm on fire.

He clears his throat, shifting his weight uncomfortably on his feet before taking a step away from me. The way he recoils has the pit of my stomach rolling. It's nothing new, so I shouldn't be surprised by the way he acts toward me. I've always seemed to have this effect on Sterling Barrett. Like something about me disgusts him.

"I'm fine, thanks," I respond, a smile plastered to my face as I look up at him without showing the pain that he causes me. This is the expectation everyone has always had of me because it's the only way I know how to act. It's easier to put on a happy face and not let the world see the ugly inside me.

There's enough ugliness in the world around us. It just always made more sense to try and add some brightness to everyone's lives.

Sterling grunts and I'm not sure if he was attempting to respond. Whatever it was, it was completely incoherent and I feel awkward as hell standing here with him right now. I'm still smiling at him as I readjust my backpack.

"Well, I should probably get going," I tell him as I begin to walk away. "I need to go find something to eat or grocery shop or something."

Sterling is silent for a moment as I begin to walk away before I hear him call out my name.

"Olivia, wait."

My breath catches in my throat at the sound of my name on his tongue. Inhaling deeply, I slowly turn around to face him as he stalks toward me. "Yeah?"

His jaw clenches for a moment, his throat bobbing as he swallows hard. "Did you want to go get food somewhere?"

A grin spreads across my face. "I would like that."

CHAPTER TWO
STERLING

I don't know why I offered to do this. I've known Olivia for a long-ass time and I can see right through the facade that she puts on. She might think that she can fool everyone else with her sunshine and happy-go-lucky attitude, but not me. I never cared much before to look beyond what she shows the world.

But behind her grin, I could see the disappointment and how uncomfortable she felt.

The least I could do was take my sister's best friend out to get some food.

Judging by how thin she is, I'm afraid if she doesn't eat, she may wither away anyway. Olivia has always been slender, it's the way that I remember her growing up. She kept my sister on track because she was the good one out of the two. While Stella wanted to get drunk and hook up with guys, Olivia was the sound voice. The angel on her shoulder.

But she was always my little sister's best friend. I could never look at her as anything more... even if she did look like a fucking angel.

"I'm going to be honest," Olivia speaks, her voice light as we begin to walk together down the sidewalk. "I haven't really ventured out much, so I'm not familiar with the restaurants around here."

Fighting the urge to look at her, I continue to walk. "What are you hungry for?"

"How about you surprise me? I'd eat just about anything right now."

"Okay," I respond quietly, not offering any more. Without thinking, I continue to walk, knowing that there's a diner only two blocks away. From the corner of my eye, I see Olivia as she wraps her arms tighter around her body. She's still carrying her backpack and the temperature continues to drop, given it's January.

I'm an asshole.

"Come with me," I tell her, reaching out to grab her arm instinctively. Olivia glances down at my hand on her and I quickly pull away from her. *What the fuck is wrong with me?* Clearing my throat, I motion for her bag. "Let me carry that for you."

We're standing in the middle of the sidewalk, Olivia's eyes widening as she stares back at me with different hues of brown and green swirling in her irises. "Okay," she replies tentatively as she shrugs the straps off her shoulders and hands it to me. "Where are we going?"

"You're cold," I say matter-of-factly as I begin to walk into the parking lot. "I'll drive."

I hear Olivia's footsteps behind me as she attempts to keep up with my longer strides. A sigh slips from my lips as I slow down my pace, allowing her to catch up to me. We walk in silence to my car and it's uncomfortable.

Olivia is the same girl that I remember from when we were younger, except she's older now. She thinks that I didn't notice her as she entered high school and began to mature, but she's wrong. I saw her. I've always seen Olivia fucking Davis.

And that's what bothers me the most.

I'm not allowed to see her. She's entirely off-limits, so it's best if I keep her at arm's length. The less she knows about me, the better. There's no room for Olivia in my life, because if I let her in, I know that she would consume me.

Olivia walks around the front of the car as I unlock the doors and slip in behind the steering wheel. I could have been a gentleman and opened her door for her, but that's not me. At least, not in this situation. The last thing I need is for her to think that this is something more than it is.

It's not a goddamn date. This is just a favor to my sister. Keep an eye on Olivia and make sure that she's good. And I suppose that making sure she's fed falls under that.

As I turn the key, starting the engine, I reach down and crank up the heat. Olivia notices the button by her seat and turns on the seat warmer. She nestles deeper against the leather cushion as she puts on her seat belt like the good girl she is.

There isn't a wild bone in this girl's body. She's as safe as they come.

"So, you didn't tell me where we were going," she reminds me, her voice soft as I pull the car out of the parking lot.

With one hand on the wheel and the other resting on the gearshift, I keep my eyes on the road instead of looking at her. "Jenny's."

I feel her curious eyes on the side of my face. "Wait, you're taking me to someone's house to eat? Who is Jenny? Your girlfriend?"

She's gained my attention now. Half turning my head to look at her, I raise an eyebrow. "Do you always have to ask so many questions?"

"If I want to know anything, then yes." She pauses for a moment, a frustrated breath slipping from her plump lips. "I like to know what I'm getting myself into or what to expect."

Choosing to not respond, I direct my gaze back to the road as an awkward silence settles between us once again. I know how Olivia is and what to expect with her. At least there's one thing about her that hasn't changed.

We're both quiet as I head away from campus and into town. I glance at her from the corner of my eye, noticing her as she thoughtfully stares out the window. I like the silence, when she's not asking a million different questions, but I want to know what is going on in that pretty little head of hers in this moment. She really thinks that I'm taking her to another girl's house for dinner.

It's a relatively short drive into town to the small diner. I don't come here that often, but it's a place where you can get amazing comfort food. And right now, that's what it looks like Olivia needs. Some kind of comfort, something to make her feel safe here, like she made the right choice moving here from Florida.

She didn't.

But I can't tell her that.

As we pull into the parking lot, I park directly in front of the small restaurant. There's a massive neon sign above that says the name... Jenny's. Putting the car in park, I kill the engine as I look over at Olivia whose hand is frozen on her seat belt.

Her bright eyes meet mine. "Oh," she says quietly, the relief heavy in her tone. "Jenny's is a diner... not your girlfriend."

I stare back at her for a moment, a million different responses racing through my brain, but instead I choose to remain silent. My lips are pressed together as I tear my gaze away from hers and climb out of the car. Olivia isn't far behind me and I hear her door slamming shut behind her as she shuffles after me.

We reach the door and I hold it open for her, our gazes colliding once more before we step inside. Her throat bobs as she swallows hard before choosing to step inside the busy restaurant.

"You might have everyone fooled with your mask of optimism, Liv," I murmur as she walks past me, catching a whiff of her light floral scent. "But not me."

CHAPTER THREE
OLIVIA

Sitting across from Sterling in this small booth is an interesting experience. Part of me doesn't feel like this is real life. There were many years where I was close to him because he was always around when I was with his sister. That was until he got older and we were too immature and just annoying to be around.

I was always his little sister's best friend, but right now, it doesn't feel quite like that. Don't get me wrong, everything about this situation is awkward and strange. He checked up on me because of Stella. She wasn't the reason why he brought me here. I'm still not sure why he extended the invitation but something in that moment made him offer us sharing a meal.

It's nothing more than that—just like it's always been.

I had the biggest crush on him when I started to get into boys, but that's all it was. Just a silly little crush. He was older, mysterious, and one hundred percent off-limits. Those three factors made him very compelling. He was popular in our school and all of the girls wanted him. Sterling always had a different girl with him.

I guess it comes with the territory, being a hotshot hockey player from our small town. That part of him was never what sucked me in. It was the way that Sterling could be gentle and caring, of course while no one else noticed. He gave me the cold shoulder when anyone else was around, but there were a few moments when it was just the two of us.

In those moments, he wasn't my best friend's asshole brother. He was more like a peer, like we were equals. Dare I even say... friends? It was one thing that always messed with my head because I couldn't question him on it. Sterling wouldn't hesitate to shut it down, to make it seem like I was the one being delusional.

And maybe I was being delusional. One side of Sterling was a lie and I can't pinpoint which one it was. The one side who found me repulsive and annoying or the side who wanted to make sure that I was safe. The side that actually listened to me and cared.

"Thanks for bringing me here," I tell Sterling as we both look over the menus in front of us. He seems to be absentmindedly staring at his, as if he's not actually looking at the words. "I would have probably just ended up in the dining hall again, since I haven't figured out the lay of the land here yet."

Sterling lifts his gaze to mine as he folds his menu closed and sets it on the table. "You don't have to thank me, Olivia."

I stare back at him for a moment, waiting for him to say something else, but his lips close and I know that he's done. Of course I have to thank him. He didn't have to do this for me tonight, but he did anyway. And I know that he could have been doing a million other things. He's always seemed disgusted and annoyed with me so I'm sure this isn't on the top of his to-do list.

"Well, hey, handsome," a girl's voice breaks through the silence between us. I glance over at our server, reading her name tag as she stares at Sterling like he created Earth. She places her hand on his shoulder as she opens her mouth again. "I wasn't sure when I would see you again."

Sterling's gaze lingers on mine for a moment, a shadow passing over his face. I feel the heat creeping up my neck and spreading across my cheeks. Tearing my eyes away from his, I stare back at the words on the menu, unable to focus on any of the words in front of me. This is beginning to feel like an intimate moment and I'm most definitely an outsider.

"Hey, Hannah," Sterling responds, directing his attention to her. I don't miss the shift in him. He's still the same grumpy asshole, but he knows how to be charming. He's cold and standoffish, but it does nothing to send girls running in the opposite direction. "Can we get two waters?"

"You can get whatever you want, baby," she murmurs, pushing her ass out as she purposely leans over the table. Her boobs look like they're going to spill out of the top of her low-cut shirt. I swallow back the bile that rises in my throat and fight the urge to vomit at how forward she is with him. It's nothing new, watching girls throw themselves at him, but Jesus Christ. He must have his claws in deep.

I meet Sterling's gaze. Something sinister plays

in his irises as he looks back at Hannah, a smirk tugging on the corners of his lips. I don't belong here. If I knew this was what I was walking into, I would have gladly eaten some ramen noodles that I had stashed in my room.

"What are you doing later tonight?" he asks her, his voice as smooth as silk.

"That depends." Hannah stands up straight, her dark brown hair spilling down her back. She glances at me, her mocha eyes meeting mine. "Who's the girl?"

I stare back at Sterling. A storm brews in the depths of his pupils as his jaw clenches. "She's just my little sister's friend."

His words are like a punch to my gut and a painful reminder.

I will never be anything more than that in Sterling Barrett's mind.

Tuning the two of them out, I wish that the ground beneath me would open up and swallow me whole. Sterling makes plans with the girl that he's obviously been involved with before, before she disappears to get our waters. The uncomfortable silence is back and my appetite has vanished.

"She seems nice," I practically choke on the words as I force them out. My mind doesn't tolerate silence well and if I'm stuck here with Sterling until he takes me home, then there's no way it can continue to be this awkward.

A soft chuckle rumbles in Sterling's chest. The sound sounds foreign to my ears, like a distant memory. And if I wasn't paying attention, it was quiet enough to go unnoticed. "You're a terrible liar, Davis."

There's a playfulness in his tone, a glimmer in his eyes that dances as he watches me with a smile threatening to consume his lips.

"I mean..." My voice trails off for a moment before a giggle slips from me. I shrug for good measure. Now is my chance to recover from the awkwardness, from seeming to be affected by their interaction. "She's pretty and didn't seem like she's mean."

Sterling raises an eyebrow. "She's no different than the rest."

"What does that mean?"

We're interrupted by Hannah as she returns with our waters, setting them down in front of us. She flirts with Sterling again, laying it on thick. It takes her longer than it should to get our order before she disappears from the table again.

"They're all the same, Olivia," Sterling says, his

voice soft as he stares through me. "There's always a mutual agreement and they're just looking for the same thing as me. None of them will ever really matter."

"Why not?" I question him, unable to stop the words before they come out. He has my curiosity piqued. It isn't often that Sterling reveals any of his cards and his comment has me wondering what really goes on inside of his mind. I want to know everything that he will give me, even if it's little breadcrumbs.

Sterling continues to stare at me, a wave of something indistinguishable passing through his eyes. "Because they're—" He pauses for a moment, his jaw tightening as he swallows roughly. "Just because, Olivia."

He's practically saved by the bell, as if he secretly called for Hannah and she just so happens to show up at our table at the perfect time with our food. Swallowing back the rest of my questions, I drop it. I already pushed him too far by bothering to ask why. None of it makes sense to me, but maybe that's the way it's supposed to be.

Sterling doesn't want to let me in and I have no choice but to accept that.

Even if it is a bitter pill to swallow.

CHAPTER FOUR
STERLING

"What's going on with you, man?" Vaughn asks me as I sit on the couch, staring at the black screen on the TV. We came back from practice instead of going out with some of the other guys and I've literally been sitting here since. Simon jumped in the shower and Vaughn disappeared into the other room before coming back in to find me like this. I haven't moved or made an attempt to grab the remote. "You've been weird as shit this past week."

I turn my head to look at him, feeling partially like a zombie. "I'm good. Just have a lot of shit on my mind."

Vaughn walks over to the couch with a bottle of water in his hand as he sits down on the other side of the sectional. "If it has anything to do with me moving in, I can get my own place. I know that you and Simon are pretty close, so I'm kind of like the third wheel being here."

"Nah." I shake my head dismissively. "It has nothing to do with that. You're practically family now since you are a part of our team. And you aren't a douchebag, at least that I've seen so far."

"So, what's really going on then?" Simon's voice breaks through as he walks into the room. I didn't even realize that he was done in the shower, but now he's in the living room with Vaughn and me.

Simon and I have been close since freshman year. He's always been more of an open book than I am. I'm usually not the one who has any problems that need discussed, so it isn't often that I need to let anyone in. Whether they're friends or family. Stella is really the only one who I talk to about shit and she's the last fucking person that I can go to about what's going on right now.

"Just some shit with my sister..." *Sister's best friend.*

Simon tilts his head to the side. He met Stella a few times when she came to stay with us. He's seen the party animal side of her and how she can get a little out of hand. I've talked to him before about how she's always been. "Is she getting into trouble in California?"

"No, she's good. Just some other shit."

He nods, finally picking up on my cues to let it go. That's one thing that Simon is good for. He knows when to stop pushing and just let it be. I'll figure it out on my own and don't need someone else to help me figure out my problems.

Honestly, this isn't even really a problem. It's just me getting inside my own head. If I can keep my distance from Olivia, then I don't have to worry about her clouding my thoughts like this. The more distance, the better. Why can't I just go back to fucking looking at her like she's my little sister's best friend instead of the woman she's grown into?

What the fuck is wrong with me?

"Okay, so if we're not going to talk about your sister, can we at least turn on the TV?" Vaughn widens his eyes, a chuckle escaping him. "I mean, let's be real. We're sitting here in silence and you're staring at the screen like there's something on there to look at."

A grin forms on my lips and I lean forward, grabbing the remote before throwing it at him. "Fuck off," I grumble, rolling my eyes as I rise to my feet. "I'm gonna get a shower anyways."

"That's probably for the best. I don't know how you've been sitting out here still smelling your stink from practice earlier."

I shrug. "We spend a lot of hours smelling like gross hockey equipment."

Vaughn scrunches up his nose. "Still doesn't make it any better."

Turning my back to him, I hear the TV click on as I head toward the staircase that leads upstairs. I head up into my room and grab a change of clothes before heading into the bathroom. I lock the door behind me before turning on the water and stripping out of the shorts and shirt I put on after practice.

This week has been a weird one. I haven't felt right after that night at the diner with Olivia. She asks too many questions and I can't stand it— mainly because I can't give her the answers she wants. They're the ones that I'm forced to keep to myself.

I know she wasn't fond of knowing that Hannah was someone I sleep with occasionally. And Hannah was practically marking her territory because the threat was there. Part of me felt like an idiot for not making her stop, but the logical part of my brain knew it was what had to be done.

Hannah is a girl that I can be involved with. She's not looking for anything more. There aren't any complications or any outside forces that could ruin it all. It's easy and simple. Olivia is complicated and I don't need that in my life. I'm so close to reaching my dream that I can't afford to lose focus now.

The NHL is literally just one step away. I've worked too hard for too long to risk jeopardizing any of that. Not that Olivia would jeopardize that, but she could fuck up a lot of things in my life. I don't know why I'm even having thoughts like this. So, what if she grew up to be a fucking bombshell? Why can't I just let my brain appreciate the way she looks and stop thinking about the fact that I know the real Olivia Davis.

I can't like her; I can't look at her like this now. Back then, it was different because I knew that nothing could happen between us. But now... now could be so different. Except it can't. I can't go there with her and I most definitely cannot develop any feelings for her.

Goddammit.

My phone buzzes from the pocket of my shorts on the floor. I pick it up and unlock the screen as I check my messages. It's one from Hannah and she wants to hang out since I blew her off the other night. I stare at my phone for a moment, contemplating the distraction. I could respond and she would be over here before I even get out of the shower.

A sigh slips from my lips and I lock my screen, not answering her before I set my phone down on the counter. While I had dinner with Olivia last week, I made plans with Hannah while we were at the diner. I dropped Olivia back off at her dorm and I just couldn't bring myself to hang out with Hannah afterward.

I don't know what the hell was wrong with me, but I completely blew her off. I've successfully been able to avoid her since then. She sent me some unsavory text messages that evening, but I haven't heard from her since. And now here she is again, offering a distraction from the shit going on in my head right now.

Stepping into the shower, the hot water burns my skin as it rolls down my back. It's like a full-body cleanse as I walk in until it's pouring down over my head, streaming down my face. I close my eyes, inhaling deeply, feeling the droplets of water hanging heavily in the steam that surrounds me.

Grabbing the shampoo, I scrub the sweat from

my hair before running it back under the water. As good as it feels, as refreshed as it's making me, it still isn't helping with the thoughts that linger in the darkest places of my mind.

I keep finding myself drifting back to Olivia and how badly I wish that I could have taken her home instead of making plans with Hannah.

My cock throbs and I'm as hard as a rock as I entertain the thoughts in my mind. She's so sweet, so innocent. Like a petite slice of heaven, wrapped in a ray of sunshine. I'd be willing to bet that no one has ever touched Olivia. And I swear to God if I find out that anyone did, I will gladly remove his hands from his body.

I know that I will never get the chance to touch her, but that doesn't mean that I can't fantasize about it. The way that her perfectly taut body would be positioned under mine. My name falling from her lips as I slide inside of her. Those plump fucking lips that I want to slide my tongue between.

If only I could just kiss her, to feel how soft her mouth is against mine. And I imagine her tasting as sweet as she is.

Somewhere while the thoughts drifted into my mind, my hand found my cock. Glancing down, I see that I'm subconsciously stroking it to the thought of

Olivia taking it deep inside her. Leaning forward in the water, it streams down my face as I plant my other hand against the shower wall and begin to stroke the length of my erection.

Olivia fucking Davis. The girl of my dreams since high school. And the one that I'll never be able to touch. Closing my eyes, I imagine her on her knees in front of me. It's her hand wrapped around me instead of my own as she takes me into her mouth. She's warm and wet and her tongue feels like fucking silk as it slides under my cock.

Jesus fucking Christ.

Sliding my hand into her hair, I grip her locks close to her scalp as she moves her head back and forth, stroking my length with her mouth. Her lips are tight around me and I'm already so fucking close. She pumps her hand faster, my hips beginning to buck as I thrust into her, and she moves her mouth along my cock.

My balls constrict, drawing closer to my body as the warmth begins to spread through my system. I can't hold it in anymore. She fucks me with her mouth and I thrust into her once more before I'm coming. My orgasm tears through my body as I come fucking harder than I have in a long time. I'm still riding the high from my climax as I open my eyes and am brought back to reality.

Olivia isn't on her knees in front of me. My hand is wrapped around my cock, slowly milking out the rest of my cum instead of her. And my cum is on the wall of the shower instead of in her mouth. A frustrated sigh slips from my lips as I release my dick. Curling my hand into a fist, I hammer it against the tiled wall of the shower, the water still streaming down my face.

I just jerked off in the shower, fantasizing about my little sister's best friend.

Of course it was just a fantasy, but fuck me for wishing it were reality.

CHAPTER FIVE
OLIVIA

As I finish my last class of the day, I'm exhausted. I came to Wyncote because of their program being better, but I wasn't fully prepared for how much work that entailed. I'm grateful that my parents have been making sure that I'm well taken care of while I'm here, because there's no way that I could manage having to work a job on top of all the schoolwork I have.

"Hey! Olivia, right?" I hear someone say as I'm walking through the doorway and into the hall. Stopping just outside the door, I turn around to see a guy that I've noticed in my class heading toward me with a smile on his face.

"Hey," I respond, shifting my weight nervously on my feet as I look up at him. His eyes are a deep green, almost the same color as ivy leaves. "Yeah, I'm Olivia," I tell him stupidly and instantly want to slap my palm against my forehead.

"I'm Noah," he says, flashing his perfectly straight teeth as he holds his hand out to me. Tentatively, I take it and lightly shake it. "I haven't seen you around before. Are you new here this semester?"

I nod, pulling my hand away from him as my skin tingles from his warmth. "I transferred here from a university in Florida. I'm a biology major."

"Oh, cool," he says with more enthusiasm than I expected. "I am too, which is probably why we're in the same class," he adds, chuckling softly.

Even though I've noticed him in class, this is the first time I'm really looking at him. His facial features are sharp, almost perfectly symmetrical. His sand colored hair is shaved on the sides and a mess of tousled waves on the top. I never noticed how good-looking he was until this very moment.

"I don't want to make this seem weird, but a few of us are getting together later to go bowling and I was wondering if you wanted to come along with us."

I stare back at him for a moment, caught off guard. My eyebrows pull together. "But you don't even know me."

That damn grin is back on his face and I hate the way it makes my stomach flip. "I've seen you around and it seems like you keep to yourself. It sucks not knowing anyone and I just thought maybe you'd want to make some friends. They're all cool, I swear." He holds up his hand in a Scout's honor salute.

He is right. Since I've been here, I haven't made a single friend, outside of my roommate. And it's not like we hang out. I've been keeping to myself because I'm too shy to approach anyone. I never know how to go about it, but now I'm glad that Noah decided to approach me.

"You know what, that actually sounds like it would be a lot of fun."

I'm nervous, walking into a situation where I don't know anyone. My anxiety likes to be prepared and know what to expect. This is completely out of my comfort zone, but I feel like I need to take that step. If I don't like it, I just won't do it again. It's time that I make a conscious effort to do something different and push myself outside of my little box of safety I've been living in for so long.

"Sweet!" Noah begins to walk, motioning for me to follow along with him. We fall into step beside each other as we head toward the south exit of the building. Noah tells me about the five other people that are going to be there, but I'm too overwhelmed to catch their names. Plus, I do better when I can put a face to a name. It helps me to remember better.

"So, I'll see you at seven at Leisure Lanes?" Noah asks me as we stop in the middle of the sidewalk outside of the dorms. His is in a different building than mine, so this is where we end for now. "Do you know where it's at?"

I shake my head, a nervous smile on my lips. "I haven't gotten to explore much other than the campus yet, but I can use my Google Maps app and find it."

Noah purses his lips, looking displeased. "Nonsense. I'll meet you out here around six forty-five and I'll drive us. It's a few blocks away, but it's too cold at night to walk that far."

I silently thank him. Needing a car is one of the downfalls of moving here from Florida. I went there without one and am now waiting for my mom to come visit and bring my car from home here. Until then, my options are either walking or Ubers. Or coming across someone who happens to have a car.

My mind drifts to Sterling and I fight hard to shove the thoughts away. I can't let my brain go there, not after seeing him last week. That night felt partially disastrous and I have no desire in revisiting that memory.

"I'll see you then," I smile at Noah, giving him a wave before disappearing into my building. My footsteps feel lighter, even though my heart pounds erratically in my chest from the anxiety that races through my system. There's a lingering feeling that maybe I should just cancel, but it's too late. I don't even have Noah's number and I'm not going to ghost him.

As much as my anxiety can get in the way, I'm not in the habit of letting people down or disappointing them. Call me a people pleaser. I just want to make sure that everyone is happy with all of the bad things in the world. Kindness is the least that I can offer to everyone that I cross paths with.

Unlike Sterling. Some people just aren't designed to be happy, I suppose. I don't know what happened to him. He didn't have a bad life and there was nothing tragic that I know of that happened to him. Maybe it's just me, because the more that I think about it, it seems like his negative feelings are directed toward me more than anyone else.

Don't get me wrong, Sterling doesn't really seem like he gives a shit about many people. He's always indifferent and never truly seems interested. Almost like he's in his own world and there isn't enough room in it to fully let someone else in. But at the same time, he's more colder toward me compared to other people.

And I really don't like the cold.

After we ate at the diner, he dropped me off at my dorm and that was the last I heard from him. I could have sworn that I saw him in the hallway the other day, but it was just from behind and he was gone before I had the chance to approach him. Not that I would have anyway. What could I have possibly said to him?

He might not have a girlfriend, but he definitely has a girl that has his attention.

And like it's always been... it isn't me.

———

Noah is already waiting for me outside when I leave the dorm building. He greets me with a smile on his face, his scarf wrapped tightly around his neck to block out the cold. I settled with a pair of thick leggings, a sweater, boots and my long down jacket. Winters in Vermont are no joke. We don't get inches of snow here, we get feet.

There's been quite a few times where I've

wondered if I made a mistake coming back here over the past week. Between the cold from the climate here and the coldness I experienced from Sterling, I miss the warmth.

Although, with the way that Noah is looking at me right now, I can't help but feel like the sun is touching my bare skin. There's something about him that makes me feel at ease, like I can be comfortable around him. Perhaps it's the warmth that he offers. He reminds me of the Florida sun in the middle of the day.

Bright and warm. He matches my energy.

"You ready to go?" he asks me, his voice soft and gentle.

"Yep," I smile back at him and follow him into the parking lot to where his car is. It's not a date, but he still opens the passenger-side door for me. He waits until I'm situated in my seat before closing it and making his way over to his side.

The leather seat is cold beneath my clothes and Noah turns up the heat as soon as he turns on the car. He doesn't have seat warmers, but it doesn't take long for his car to warm up. We fall into a comfortable conversation on our way to the bowling alley, talking about our plans after graduation. We still have three years to go until we're at that point and so much can change before then.

It doesn't take long before we're at the bowling alley and Noah is putting the car in park. I climb out of my door and wait for him, nervously wringing my hands together. He offers me a kind smile as he comes up beside me and we walk inside together. His friends already have two lanes and are waiting for us when we get there.

My nerves instantly fade as everyone goes around, introducing themselves to me. There are two couples, Eric and Sam and Jay and Darla. And then the only other one who isn't coupled up, Steven. I can't help but feel like Noah brought me here as his date, but I quickly push the irrational thoughts from my mind.

He hasn't once made an attempt to make this seem like it's anything more than it is. Leave it to me to overthink and jump to conclusions. Everyone is welcoming and extremely nice, asking me questions like they genuinely want to get to know me.

"You're a biology major too, right?" Sam asks me as we watch Eric and Jay both bowl. I'm sitting with Sam and Darla while Noah and Steven argue about football teams.

"I am." I smile back at her. "I just transferred to

Wyncote this semester and met Noah in one of the classes we have together."

"Watch out for that one," Darla winks at me. "He's quite the charmer, but he's got a good head on his shoulders."

"Oh no." I shake my head at her, quickly shutting down the idea. "We literally just met. We're friends, if we're anything at all."

Sam laughs softly. "Don't listen to Darla. She's been on him to get a girlfriend, but Noah isn't really like that. He's super focused on his schooling."

"You're not crazy, right?" Darla questions me, a smile playing on her lips.

I shake my head, laughing with the two of them. "Not that I know of."

"Good, because I like you. And I think I like you for him."

Sam rolls her eyes at Darla before looking back at me. "Like I said, don't listen to her. She's always trying to play matchmaker."

"Hey, I did hook you and Eric up, didn't I?"

Sam raises her hands in defeat. "Okay, okay, you got me there."

"Damn right," Darla winks at me, laughing again. "Let me work my matchmaker magic. I promise I won't do you wrong."

"I'm not looking for a relationship or anyone right now, honestly," I tell her, swallowing back the nervousness that creeps up into my throat. All while simultaneously shoving thoughts of Sterling from my mind.

"Okay, I'll back off... for now." Darla smiles at me. "But if we're going to be friends, I can't promise that I won't try again."

Noah walks over to the three of us. "Are the two of you harassing Olivia?"

The three of us laugh and Darla and Sam shake their heads in an attempt to look innocent. "We would never do such a thing," Darla says sweetly.

"Yeah right," Noah snorts. "I know the two of you and the way you work." Noah looks back at me, holding his hand out to help me up. "It's your turn."

I smile at him, sliding my hand into his as I feel his warm palm against mine.

And I really like the warmth.

CHAPTER SIX
STERLING

I sit in the parking lot after finishing my last class of the day. I have approximately fifteen minutes to get to the rink and onto the ice for practice. Yet, I can't seem to get myself to move my car. I've been sitting here waiting for a glimpse of her.

Call me crazy, a stalker, whatever the fuck you want. In the past week, I've only seen Olivia two times and each was from a distance. And each time, I saw her with some dickhead. I don't know who the hell he is, but I have every intention of finding out.

When I saw the two of them together, they were walking into a classroom side by side. It shouldn't be hard to figure out who he is, if they have a class together. I don't give two fucks about that. What I do give a fuck about is the way they didn't seem like they were just two students going into the same room who didn't know each other.

They're friends.

Or something more... which only makes my blood boil.

Olivia isn't mine. She can't be. But if she ends up being someone else's, I don't know if I want to see that. She's too good—way too good for anyone that I could possibly imagine. She has a sunshine personality, but that doesn't come close to touching her. *Olivia is the fucking sun.*

Grabbing onto the gearshift, I'm about to put my car in reverse when I catch sight of her walking down the sidewalk. She's alone and my stomach does a weird somersault that I'm not particularly fond of. I like her alone, away from anyone else. She's safer that way, not only physically, but her heart is safe as well.

I pause for a moment, about to lift my foot off the brakes, when I see Olivia's dark hair whip around her body as she spins on her heel. My eyes follow the direction she's looking in. And I fucking see him. The same dickhead I saw her walking with into class.

Anger laces through my veins and my knuckles

turn white as I grip the steering wheel and gearshift tighter.

He's sporting a huge grin on his face as he jogs over to her and I want to slap the look from his face. I watch the two of them, unable to hear anything they're saying. They turn to continue walking, but they're walking in my direction. Olivia keeps looking over at him, her face shining brightly.

And I hate the way she's looking at him right now.

The way her head tips back with laughter, her smile reaching her eyes.

I don't know who the hell he is, but I do know one thing...

He's got to go.

———

My skates glide effortlessly across the freshly cleaned ice. We've been through our warm-ups already and everyone is lining up for the puck drop. It's not our first game of the season, but this one feels different. It isn't often that I go into one already feeling pissed off, like I'm ready to be out for blood.

Hell, that isn't even my position when I play. I'm not one of the enforcers. I'm not the player that our coach sends out when it's time to fuck up someone else. But I need to take this aggression out on someone. The adrenaline is in full force, coursing through my veins, and I'm ready to play my ass off.

I get into position, watching Vaughn as he lines up with the center from the other team. He and August play the same position and Coach has been trying to divide the ice time between them equally. With his high level of skill, there's a possibility that he could outskate us, which says a lot. None of us are jealous of him, though. He's a part of our team, so the support is endless.

Both of them are slightly crouched, their sticks on the ice waiting for the puck to land between the two of them. The ref drops it and skates backward, out of the way, as Vaughn and the other player fight over it. Vaughn wins the face-off and passes the puck to Logan. He ends up skating with it before passing it to Cam who then sends it off to Vaughn again.

Vaughn manages to send the puck soaring through the goaltender's legs, a five-hole shot. Instead of going over to him to celebrate, I have my sights set on the motherfucker who checked me during the last game we played. I skate toward him at full speed, my skates slicing through the ice as I stop abruptly in front of him when he turns to face me.

Dropping my stick, I shove my hands against his chest. His eyebrows draw together as his eyes slice to mine. He slides backward for a moment but quickly recovers.

"What the fuck?" he snarls at me, dropping his own stick to the ground. "You want to fucking go?"

"Does it look like I'm here to talk?" I flick my wrists, tossing my gloves onto the ice as I square up with him.

"It was a clean hit from the last game," he argues, not fully taking the bait. He's silent for a moment before he tosses his own gloves onto the ice beside him. "Fuck it. You wanna go, let's do it."

"What the hell are you doing, Barrett?" I hear Cam's voice from somewhere around us. All I can think of right now is ripping off this guy's helmet and driving my fist into his face.

We're both squared up, skating around each other for a fraction of a second, before he comes at me. He throws a punch, hitting me in the ribs where there's no padding. My lungs constrict in protest, but the adrenaline completely washes it away as I rush at him. Grabbing the cage of his helmet, I violently twist it until the snaps on the sides are popping off.

He throws another fist, hitting me in the side of my head that is still covered by my helmet as I proceed to rip his off. It falls onto the ice by our feet and my gaze meets his. Except, it's not the player from the team that I'm seeing anymore. My mind creates a mirage and the other player morphs into the fucking asshole that I saw with Olivia. Curling my fingers into my palm, I raise my arm and drive my fist under his jaw.

His head jerks upward, blood flying from his mouth as he bites down on his lip from the force. I can't think straight in this moment. All I want to do is beat the hell out of this guy, but not really him. I'm channeling all my anger, my feelings, my emotions, and taking it out on a guy who didn't even do anything dirty to me.

In an instant, he's rushing into me, his shoulder slamming into my chest as he attempts to take me down onto the ice. My arms slide under his, locking him in place as I gain my footing. We struggle against each other. Slipping my leg around the back of his, I force his knee to bend as he loses his balance and falls onto the ice.

Just as I'm about to hit him again, someone's

pulling him away from me as the ref is forcing himself between the two of us. I'm back on my skates, spinning around with the anger still racing through my system, mixing with the adrenaline. Vaughn, Logan, and Cam are standing there staring at me.

Hayden isn't far behind them, sliding to a stop by me. "Dude, what the fuck are you doing?"

I glance between the four of them, my chest heaving with every breath I take as the adrenaline continues to rock my system. Turning back to the guy I just punched, I see the blood on his face and I instantly know that I'm fucked. I saw it in the moment, but it didn't register in my mind until now.

"They're going to throw you out of the game," Cam points out with a scowl on his face. "You do realize that, right?"

"You're lucky if they don't suspend you for a few games," Hayden adds.

I look to Logan for some kind of guidance. If there's anyone who gets into fights frequently, it's him. Although, his situations are typically different. He's smart about the way he goes about it. He doesn't act like a goddamn psychopath like I just did.

Logan frowns. "I don't know, man. I've gotten

suspended before, but that's why I've learned to fight smarter than that." He pauses for a moment, his voice dropping. "Are you good? This isn't like you at all."

"Barrett!" our coach yells my name from the bench. "Get your ass over here, right now!"

My stomach sinks and I hang my head in defeat as I leave the guys behind me and head over to where our coach is standing. This is why I don't let my emotions get involved. They do nothing but cause problems.

And I may have just completely fucked myself over.

CHAPTER SEVEN
OLIVIA

Class wraps up and our professor is finally dismissing us with a report that is due in two weeks. It's not a huge one, but it's still a pretty hefty assignment that I need to get a good grade on. Noah waits for me by the door as I gather my belongings and shove them into my bag. After clearing my desk, I head over to him, a grin tugging on the corners of my lips.

"You want to go get lunch?" Noah asks me as he holds the door open for me. "When is your next class?"

"I actually have the rest of the afternoon off."

We fall into step with one another, wading through the sea of students. Mondays are thankfully my easy days. I only have classes in the mornings and then after lunch, my afternoon is free. This would probably be the time that I could use to find a job. Although, my parents have been making my transition into college simpler by sending me money when I need it.

"Damn." Noah frowns as we walk down the steps into the main entrance to the building. "I literally have a half hour break and then classes until dinnertime. Did you want to run to the café to grab something to eat?"

I hear Noah speaking, but I'm not fully listening to him. Hell, I'm not even looking at him—I'm looking past him, but he doesn't seem to notice. I'm completely distracted, but my distraction has a name.

Sterling Barrett.

And he's standing with some of his friends with his famous scowl. His eyes ignite, a fire burning inside of them as he narrows them at me. His jaw tightens, his throat bobbing as he swallows hard. He looks as if he's a statue—a pissed-off one at that.

"Olivia?" Noah breaks through my thoughts and I quickly look back up at him, knowing that there's a completely lost expression on my face. "Did you hear anything I said?"

"Yeah, sorry," I tell him, offering a polite smile as

I shrug. Glancing over Noah's shoulder, I see Sterling and his friends heading outside. His gaze meets mine once more as he throws a glance back to me before slipping through the doorway. "I—uh—I actually have something that I need to do. But tomorrow?"

Noah doesn't even appear disappointed. There isn't a single mean bone in this guy's body. He gives me a genuine smile and nods. "Sounds good. I'll see you in class tomorrow."

I'm almost shocked at the fact that he literally leaves it at that. He doesn't press for anything more, he just drops the entire conversation with the promise of seeing each other tomorrow. My feet are stuck to the floor for a moment as I watch him disappear through the side door. There was nothing malicious about how he acted.

That's just how Noah is. Warm, friendly, a people pleaser. He just always seems content with anything, as if he doesn't want to rock the boat in any way. I'm not sure how I feel about it. In a sense, I like the simplicity, the way he matches the same positivity I'm trying to put out in the world. But at the same time, I can't tell if it's superficial or not.

We all have layers, but what if that's Noah's only one? What if there's nothing beneath that and what you see is what you get? I don't like the way it messes with my mind and I know the root cause of it.

That infamous scowl that always has a way of muddling my thoughts.

An exasperated sigh slips from my lips and I turn back to the main entrance, seeing Sterling walking by himself. I don't know where his friends went, but this is my chance to approach him. My feet move quickly as I shuffle past the other students crowding the area and I step out into the cold air. The wind whips, burning my cheeks, but I ignore it as I follow behind Sterling.

"Hey, wait up!" I call out after him, but my voice gets lost in a gust of wind. Sterling doesn't hear me and continues to walk as I continue to get closer to him. Breaking out into a jog, it doesn't take me long to reach him. "Sterling," I say his name as I'm almost directly behind him.

This time he hears me. He stops, turning around to face me, just as I trip over my own feet. I hadn't planned on crashing into him, but I'm struggling to regain my footing as I begin to fall in his direction. I'm too close to him to fall onto the ground. There's no room and my only choice is to collide directly with him.

Sterling throws his arms out to catch me, just as I land against his solid chest. My breath leaves my lungs in a rush and he wraps his hands around my biceps as he holds me up. Tilting my head back, my eyes meet his and he's close... too close. The faint cedar smell of his cologne invades my senses. There's a warmth to him that reminds me of the Sterling I knew growing up.

And it instantly vanishes as I regain my footing. The softness in his expression is gone and he moves me away from him, his hands abandoning my arms as a look of torment washes over his irises. Heat creeps up my neck, spreading across my cheeks, and I want the ground to open up and swallow me whole. He seems to have that kind of effect on me.

"Are you okay?" he asks, his voice quiet as he stares back at me.

"I am," I practically whisper. "I'm sorry about that."

A ghost of a smile plays on his lips. "We need to stop running into each other like this," he half jokes and I'm almost expecting his lips to curve upward, but they don't. "If I didn't know any better, I might think that you're doing it on purpose."

"No, not at all," I admit in a rush, feeling the

embarrassment consuming me. Sterling's eyes are trained on mine as he lifts an eyebrow.

"Of course not," he agrees, a hint of irritation in his tone. "I'm sure your little boyfriend wouldn't appreciate that, now would he?"

My eyebrows tug together. "I don't have a boyfriend."

"Tell that to the asshole who keeps looking at you like you hung the sun in the sky."

I stare back at him, my eyes narrowing as his words resonate in my mind. Of course Sterling would have an issue with it. Just add that to the list of things he doesn't like. "What's so wrong with the way he looks at me? At least he can appreciate the good that I have to offer."

Sterling's jaw tics, but he reaches out, his hands finding my coat as he lifts my hood over my head against the wind. A storm brews in his irises as they focus in on mine. "Because he should be looking at you like you are the sun."

My lips part slightly, my heart constricts in my chest. Sterling drops his hands away from my coat and turns away from me. I'm frozen in place, my feet cemented to the ground as I watch him step off the curb and walk into the parking lot.

I don't understand Sterling. One minute he's as

cold as ice, ready to put as much distance between us as possible. The next minute, he's soft and warm, saying things that my soul is so desperate to hear from him. I don't know what he wants from me.

And I'm not so sure I want to know.

———

Later that evening, I'm back in my dorm room reading a book. My roommate is once again not here. It's been relatively lonely sharing a room with her since she's always at her boyfriend's. I grew up in a very loud household with three other siblings. And when I was at college in Florida, my roommate was someone I grew close to.

It's been pretty lonely, just sharing the silence with myself most of the time. I'm deep in the book that I'm reading, when my phone begins to ring. My face lights up, my mood instantly lifting as I see it's my best friend calling.

Since Stella moved to California and we both kind of went our separate ways with college, we haven't been in touch like we used to. There was a point where we didn't go a day without talking. Now, it's fizzled out to only every few weeks. Which, I'm not mad about.

I completely understand it. We both have our own separate lives now. Stella moved across the country and had no option but to make new friends. And luckily for her, she's more of an extrovert than I am. So, while it's been easy for her to make new friends, I've been the one who is struggling.

I've always been more of an introvert and kept to myself. Stella was the peanut butter to my jelly. She was the one who I could count on to help pull me out of my shell and my comfort zone. She never pushed me to do anything that I wasn't comfortable with, but she always made sure that I was trying something new instead of being stuck in my safety net ways.

"Hello," I answer, my voice lifting higher than it has been lately. I can't help but feel a sudden pang of sadness as I hear laughter in the background of wherever Stella is. I wish I were there with my best friend, living life like we always did.

"Hey, girl!" Stella's voice is loud and energetic. "How are you? I feel like we haven't talked in forever." Something shuffles around in the background and I hear a door close as she must have gone into another room. "Let's FaceTime so I can make sure you're actually good like you're going to tell me you are."

A soft laugh falls from my lips and I answer the FaceTime request as it comes through. Stella's face fills my screen and I realize in this moment just how long it's been since we last saw each other. We were supposed to get together over winter break, but she ended up staying in California instead of coming here.

"That's better," she beams, flashing her bright white smile that I haven't seen in forever. As I stare back at her, my mind can't help but drift to Sterling. The similarities between the two of them are so strong, I feel like I'm looking at his twin right now. "How are you, Liv?"

Adjusting myself on my bed, I sit up straighter, positioning my head against the headboard as I stare back into her dark brown eyes. "I've been good. Just trying to get used to being here and figuring out how to navigate this semester."

"I know you better than anyone else, Liv. You might say that you're good, but I can see past that. What's really going on?" She pauses for a moment, her lips tugging downward into a frown. "How are the people there? Have they been nice to you? Have you made any friends?"

I can't stop the laughter that falls from my lips as I shake my head at Stella. "Jeez. How about one question at a time?" I purposely avoid the comment she made about seeing past me just saying that I'm good.

Stella might know me better than most. She can tell when there's something else that's going on. I'm usually really good at keeping my mask on, creating a sunshine vibe for everyone to jive with. Stella is one of the only people that can tell that it's bullshit sometimes... the other just so happens to be her older brother.

"Okay, let's start with the first one. How are the people there?"

I shrug. "They seem to be fairly nice. I haven't run into any issues with anyone, but I've been keeping my head down and making sure that I'm worrying about my own stuff instead of what's going on with everyone else."

"What did I tell you about that?" Stella scowls, her eyebrows tugging together. "You need to branch out and make some friends. How are you going to get to know anyone if you don't go out and get the full college experience. I know that you're super focused on your classes and shit, but come on, girl. Life is completely passing you by while you're hanging out in your dorm room with your nose in a book."

"There's nothing wrong with that if it's something I enjoy doing," I argue, coming to my own defense. Usually I wouldn't fight her on it, but there's something about the way she says it that strikes a nerve. It's almost as if she's implying I'm living my life the wrong way because I'm not doing the same things she is doing. I'm doing exactly what I want to do, even if it is a little bit lonely.

"I'm not saying there is, Liv. But there's so much that college can offer you socially instead of just academically." She pauses again for a second, brushing her long dark hair away from her face. "Please tell me you've at least made one friend. What about the guys there? I know I've seen some pretty good-looking ones when I've gone to visit my brother."

"I actually have made a friend... and he is a guy."

Stella's lips part, forming an O shape as she stares at me in disbelief. "No fucking way. I need every detail immediately."

"He's just a friend. Noah. I met him in one of my biology classes. We hung out like twice, but he's literally just a friend and nothing more."

"Come on," Stella pleads, her lip pouting out. "You've got to give me more than that. Is he hot? Have you guys done anything?"

"Yes and no," I answer her, attempting to appease her without getting her hopes up that this is going somewhere with Noah.

And I'm not saying that it isn't. He's definitely someone I could see myself with. He fits the exact mold I've always imagined. Except my imagination and what my heart wants don't exactly match up. He doesn't fit the mold that my heart has already crafted for me.

He isn't Sterling.

And unfortunately, Sterling is the only one who fits that mold.

"Okay, why not?"

"I don't know," I admit—well, it's more like a half-truth. "We're just friends. I barely even know him. Other than him, the only other person I've really talked to is my roommate, and she's gone half the time."

Stella stares at me through the screen for a moment, her lips pursed as a wave of sadness passes through her eyes. "You're practically all alone there, Liv." She swallows, shaking her head. "I don't like it at all. What about my brother? He hasn't reached out to you or anything?"

Shit.

I swallow hard and completely forget about the

thought of being lonely. Instead, my mind is plagued by thoughts of him. The very ones I've been trying to avoid. I could tell her the truth about our interactions or I could keep them to myself completely.

"I've seen him around campus. We went out to get dinner one night, but that's about it."

Stella's nostrils flare, a displeasing look on her face as she frowns again. "You've only hung out once?"

I nod. "I mean, it's not like he needs to be my friend or anything. I'm sure he's super busy with hockey and his own life. Just because we grew up together doesn't mean we need to be friends."

Stella shakes her head. "Nope, I don't approve of that one bit. He's there; he's been there for three fucking years. The least he can do is befriend you until you find a few of your own."

My heart pounds erratically in my chest as panic begins to set in. I rapidly shake my head, my voice catching in my throat for a moment. "No, Stella. Don't."

"Bye, babe!" she exclaims, blowing me a kiss. "I need to talk to my brother, so I'll talk to you later. Love you!"

My lips part to get a word in, but she disconnects the call before I get a chance to say anything else to her. Slamming my lips back together, I slowly sink down deeper into the bed, feeling dread rolling in the pit of my stomach. The last thing I need is for Sterling to be around more, especially if it's out of pity.

He's already made it clear he doesn't particularly care for me, even if he wants to make sure I'm safe. He's not here to be my friend or anything like that. He's just my best friend's older brother, nothing more.

Suddenly it feels as if my safety net has been ripped away from me. Stella might think she's doing me a favor, but in reality she's only making this even worse for me. She knew when we were younger that I had a crush on her brother, but I think as soon as I got a boyfriend, she thought those feelings were gone; she never brought it up again.

She doesn't know how deep my feelings for him run.

And Stella is about to put me in the most awkward position I've ever been in before.

CHAPTER EIGHT
STERLING

"Sterling Austin Barrett. I am extremely disappointed in you."

I roll my eyes, holding my phone to my ear as my sister scolds me like she's our mother. "I did exactly what you asked me to do, Stella. You never asked me to befriend her. Just to keep an eye on her and make sure she's safe, which I have been doing."

"I don't care. You know how Liv is. She doesn't make friends so easily because she's such an introvert. She needs someone to help pull her out of her shell."

"I'm the last person who is going to pull her out of her shell. You do realize who you're talking to, right?"

Stella scoffs. "Please, Sterling. Don't act like you're not a people person. You just get a bug up your ass every now and then, and that's when you shut everyone else out. You know how to talk to people. Just make my best friend fucking happy, please?"

Inhaling deeply, I sigh. My eyes fall shut and I roll onto my back as I stare up at the ceiling in my bedroom. "And how do you propose I do that, exactly?"

"Maybe be nice to her for starters?"

It's my turn to scoff. "I am nice to her."

"Yeah, right," Stella half laughs. "I've seen how you are with Olivia before. I don't know what happened that you got such a chip on your shoulder toward her. At one point, you seemed like you enjoyed being around her and then you just went cold on her."

I swallow hard over the lump that forms in my throat. I didn't think Stella noticed. Thankfully, she isn't questioning my reasoning, but she's definitely noticed that I kept Olivia at arm's length. And if my sister knew why, I think it's safe to say that she would agree with it. She would completely understand, especially because she wouldn't want her best friend to get hurt.

And I'm fairly certain that is the only thing I would do to her.

"Okay, so what else other than being nice to her?"

Stella is silent for a moment. "Hang out with her. Take her out and show her around. She seems so goddamn lonely and I hate that for her. Can you just do me a huge favor and be a friend to her?"

My breath catches in my throat. First, she wanted me to keep an eye on Olivia and make sure she was safe. Now she wants me to be her fucking friend? How the hell is that going to work out?

It isn't.

"Look, Stell," I start, but she abruptly cuts me off.

"No way, you're not getting out of this, Sterling. I'm practically begging you. Please just make some time for my best friend and make her feel like she's not alone there?"

I fucking hate this. I hate my sister for doing this to me and for putting me in this position. She knows exactly what she's doing. She's been doing this kind of shit to me since we were kids and she knows how to take advantage of me. I've always had a hard time of telling her no and when she gets like this, it's almost like I can see my kid sister, begging me to push her on the swings or something.

I can't say no to her, even if I want to.

"Fine," I tell my sister, my voice coming out more as a sigh. I don't know whether it's from defeat or what exactly. I'm not looking forward to this for all of the wrong reasons. It has nothing to do with not wanting to make Olivia feel like she has someone here.

It's simply because I don't want to be that person for Olivia. I can't be that person because I know I can't let myself get close to her. There's something about her; there's always been something about her, and it wouldn't take much for me to fall off the edge with her.

I can't let that happen. I refuse to let that happen. And the closer I get to her, the harder it is to resist.

"Wait, really?" Stella questions me, the surprise heavy in her words. "You're just going to agree like that and not make it difficult."

"Don't make me change my mind," I warn her even though there's a lightness in my tone. I may be hard on my sister sometimes but it's for her own benefit. That doesn't mean I'm not going to give her some shit too. That's exactly what we do when we're getting along, even though some people might think we're actually being serious.

"Okay, okay. I won't push anymore." Stella pauses for a fraction of a second, yelling to someone in the background. "I gotta go, bro, but if I hear a bad report from Olivia, I'm going to come there and beat your ass myself."

A laugh rumbles in my chest. "Yeah, I'm sure you will."

Stella is almost half my size. Okay, that's an exaggeration. She and Olivia are both about the same height, which is easily a foot shorter than me. Not to mention the lifting and workouts that I have to do for hockey. The only thing Stella does to work out her lungs is smoke weed. She couldn't hurt a fly.

And knowing Olivia... sweet, soft Olivia. She wouldn't let Stella beat me up even if she is her best friend. She knows how our relationship has always been, but if there's one thing she wouldn't stand by, it's violence.

Stella ends the call with a quick goodbye and the promise of checking in with me later in the week. I don't know why she feels the need to do that. It's not like I'm not going to stand by my word. But then again, Stella knows how I am with obligations.

She just doesn't know how I am when that obligation is Olivia Davis.

The girl I can't seem to get out of my fucking head.

———

The next morning, I'm out of the house before any of the other guys, heading to campus. I know how Olivia operates. She's the type of person who would be at class waiting outside the door before it started. She's very neat and orderly. I don't know if she has some form of anxiety or what it is. She creates her own safety nets and they have to remain intact.

Getting to class early is one of her safety nets. She likes knowing what to expect and I appreciate that about her. She's smart and cautious, even if she doesn't like to live life on the wild side. That's one thing I always liked about Olivia. She was never like the other girls. Peer pressure didn't mean shit to her willpower. If she didn't want to do something, she wasn't going to do it.

And I'm not sure if hanging out with me is even something she really wants to do.

Just like I suspected, as I walk into the main building, I find Olivia sitting on a bench by herself.

She has AirPods in and her nose is buried deep in a book. She doesn't notice me when I first step inside, out of the cold. I like it that way. It isn't often that anyone can see her like this. It might seem like she's usually in her own little world, but she's constantly observing everything. There isn't a detail she doesn't take in from her surroundings.

But right now, seeing her like this... she is lost in her own little world. Nothing from the outside matters to her and I like it. I like the innocence of it all. The way her mind is captivated in some grand story, one that most likely is far from reality.

A smile tugs on my lips and I step deeper into the foyer area, heading directly toward her. I don't stop until I'm standing by her feet. Olivia lifts her head, her hazel eyes wide as they meet mine. She quickly closes her book and plucks out her AirPods as she looks up at me.

"Hi," she says softly, her voice like velvet as it slides across my eardrums. "What are you doing here?"

"I could ask you the same thing," I reply as I drop down onto the bench beside her.

"Stella put you up to this, didn't she?" Olivia questions me, turning to face me. "Look, I appreciate it, but I don't need a babysitter."

Her words feel like a knife in my chest. My sister must have talked to her before she called me. I'm not surprised with the way that Stella schemes, but I can see how it's affecting Olivia. She's uncomfortable under my gaze and now it's even more uncomfortable because she thinks that I'm just here because my sister asked me to be.

And I'm not even sure if that's the full reason why I agreed to do this.

"What if she isn't behind it? What if I'm here because I want to be?"

A harsh laugh escapes Olivia and it sounds foreign coming from her. The only laughter that I'm used to hearing slip from those beautiful lips is the kind that sounds like music to your ears. Like a melody that you feel in your soul, the kind you play on repeat.

"Yeah, right." She rolls her eyes at me, which is just as unusual for her. "I talked to Stella last night. I know she called you as soon as we got off the phone. We don't have to do this, Sterling. Let me save you from putting yourself through any misery and tell you that I'm okay with not being friends."

She completely catches me off guard. This isn't the sunshine Olivia that I'm used to and I'm not sure how to respond. It has to be from her anxiety or something, the fact that she's lashing out like this. It's an uncomfortable situation for her and I don't want her to feel like that at all. I want to be one of her safety nets, not something that causes her any anxious feelings.

"She did call me," I admit quietly as I slide my hands into the front pocket of my hoodie. "But that's not why I'm here. She doesn't like that you're practically all alone here, and I don't either."

"I'm fine, Sterling," she insists, her voice cracking. "I've made a few friends and I'm getting along here just fine. I don't need you checking in on me or feeling any type of obligation."

"And who are your friends? That douchebag you've been hanging out with?"

Olivia fights back a smile, ducking her head as she grabs her book and slides it into her bag. "Noah is a nice guy and he's just a friend, not that it concerns you."

I can't help the jealousy and irritation from the thought of the two of them together. He better not put his hands on her. They better just stay friends. Or there's a strong possibility that I may lose my mind. She may not be mine, but she's not allowed to be anyone else's.

Ignoring the comment about Noah, I switch

back to the real conversation that we were having. "Stella did ask me to make an effort to hang out with you, but she's not the reason why I'm sitting here right now. You've known me all of your life, Olivia. When have you ever known me to do something that I don't want to do?"

Olivia lifts her gaze back to mine with a thoughtful look swirling in her irises. She knows that I'm right. If I didn't want to hang out with her, I fucking wouldn't. It's that simple. I may be doing what my sister asked, but it's because, for whatever reason, I want to.

Even if I know that it's a bad idea.

I can't believe I'm fucking saying this shit, but I can't stop the words before the escape my lips. "Let me be your friend, Olivia. Even if it's just temporary. Just let me be someone who can be there for you."

Olivia stares at me before rising to her feet. "I appreciate the offer, but I know how you feel about me, Sterling. You've made it crystal clear that I'm a nuisance and you can't stand me."

She's so far off base, with no idea of how I really do feel. And I'm the asshole who has led her to believe that this is how I really feel. She abruptly spins on her heel, heading toward the staircase that leads up to the second floor. "I have to get to class," she tosses over her shoulder.

I watch for a moment, completely speechless, as she begins to ascend up the stairway. What happened to my sunshine Olivia? Or is this one of her layers that she doesn't show to the outside world? That thought alone makes my body warm, my heart swelling. She's comfortable enough with me to show one of her hidden layers.

"Olivia, wait!" I call out after her, hopping off the bench as I begin to sprint up the stairway after her. She stops in the middle, turning around to face me as I stop on the step below her. Where we're standing, it has her elevated and at eye level with me.

She stares at me, her eyes searching mine as she waits for my reasoning for running after her. I swallow roughly over the lump in my throat and shift my weight on my feet as I get lost in the depths of her eyes. I never noticed the small golden flecks that float in her irises.

"You're so far off base with how you think that I feel," I admit, my voice just barely above a whisper. I don't know what the hell I'm saying right now, but I can't stop it from coming out again. Something about her strips away my filter. "You aren't a nuisance and believe it or not, I can stand you."

"So, why are you so cold to me, Sterling?" she questions me, her eyes desperately searching mine with pain laced in them. "Why do you act like you want nothing to do with me? And now you want me to truly believe that you want to be friends and it's not just because of your sister?"

"I can't give you all the answers, Liv," I tell her, the sorrow evident in my words. "I'm sorry. If I could, I would, but I just can't... not yet, at least. I know that it's asking a lot, but can you just trust me on this?"

She's silent for a moment, staring back at me like she doesn't know what to say. "Okay," she says softly, completely catching me by surprise. "I have no reason not to trust you. That's one thing you've done right."

Another knife to the chest.

"Give me a chance to be your friend?"

She stares at me, chewing on the inside of her cheek as she considers my question. It feels like an eternity, waiting for some kind of a response from her. I don't care if she throws it in my face and attempts to reject me. She knows I won't leave it at that. My sister may have initiated this, but now I'm just rolling along with it script-free.

"Fine," she agrees with a slight hesitation in her voice. "I don't know what you mean by friends, but sure. We're friends now, Sterling."

There's something off about her. A coldness that is a stark contrast from her normal warmth. Perhaps she's just giving me a taste of my own medicine. She's letting me feel the same frigid air she's felt radiating from me whenever we're in close proximity to one another.

Her lips part as if she's going to say something else, but they quickly close and she turns away from me. I watch her lift one foot to take a step away, but I can't let that happen. Reaching out, I grab her wrist, attempting to stop her.

And it works.

Olivia stops, mid-step, and turns back to look at me. Her eyes look down to my hand wrapped around her wrist before her gaze meets mine. There are so many lingering questions but she swallows them all down. Which is another new thing for Olivia. Usually the questions flow from her like a goddamn river. I know that I should let go, but I like the way her skin feels beneath my palm.

Soft and warm, just like the Olivia I know she's hiding from me right now.

I can feel her pulse beneath my fingertips and I can't help but smile. It isn't a flashing grin, but the corners of my lips lift slightly. Holding on to her gaze, I stare directly at her.

"I want to show you around town tonight."

Olivia frowns slightly. "I have plans already."

"Cancel them."

Her eyebrows tug together. "I can't just cancel them on short notice. That's not how I am and it's rude."

"Sure you can. Do it. I'll pick you up around six and we can go explore the city."

Olivia's lips part and I release her wrist, immediately feeling her absence as I turn around and begin to walk back down the stairs. I know the longer I stay, the more she's going to try and fight me on this. She should know better; she knows I get what I want. And what I want with her is a chance to show her that I can be her friend.

"Sterling, I can't," she calls out after me.

I don't turn back around to look at her as I head back toward the front door of the building. "Six o'clock, Olivia," I tell her over my shoulder. "Be ready."

Without giving her the chance to say anything else, I head through the door and slip back into the cold morning air.

I don't give a fuck who she has plans with already.

Because she has plans with me instead now.

CHAPTER NINE
OLIVIA

My mind is distracted for the entire day by Sterling and running into him this morning. I wasn't expecting him, but I had a feeling that I would hear from him eventually after my conversation with Stella. However, this morning didn't exactly go as I expected our next interaction would be.

The side of Sterling that I saw this morning brought back a sense of nostalgia. It was the old Sterling, the one who used to be kind and caring to me when no one else was paying attention. The soft, gentle Sterling. The one who made the butterflies come to life in my stomach.

And the one that I've been trying to avoid because it just messes with my head beyond belief.

He practically cornered me this morning. I tried to turn him down because there was a part of me that felt like he was doing it out of obligation until he reminded me something about himself. Sterling Barrett doesn't do something that he doesn't want to do. Even if he felt an obligation because of Stella, he wouldn't have been as persistent if it wasn't something he actually wanted to do.

Which I don't know how to really feel about.

I don't know if I can handle the way it toys with my mind. My heart and soul get their hopes up, only to be let down when I realize that I'm reading into something more than it actually is with Sterling. I'm afraid to be friends with him because I don't know if I can be. I don't know if I'm capable of maintaining a friendship when I'm actually in love with him.

I refuse to admit it out loud, but it's the truth.

I've been in love with him since we were kids and that has never gone away or changed, even though I've tried. Lord, I have tried so hard to get him out of my head.

And here I am, having to cancel my original plans because Sterling wants to spend the evening together. As pathetic as it sounds, it wasn't really a question. I would have jumped at the opportunity without any hesitation before I met Noah.

We're just friends, but I have a sense of loyalty to him. Along with some curiosity of what could happen between us. He's someone I could have a real future with.

Sterling, on the other hand... that's always been a pipe dream. We all know how Sterling's future is going to look and I'm not quite sure I fit into the picture aside from being his sister's best friend. He's destined for greatness, whereas I will never reach the same levels as him in life. We're all just people simply living in Sterling's world.

I see Noah in the hallway, waiting for me outside of the class we have together. We were supposed to have plans tonight to go see a movie, but here I am having to cancel on him. The guilt is already there, and it's heavy as hell. He's been talking about this since last week. A new Marvel movie that I have no idea what it's about, but he was excited. And seemed even more thrilled that I agreed to go watch it with him.

"Hey, Olivia," he greets me with that infamous bright smile as I stop in front of him. "How are you?"

"I'm alright," I tell him with a shrug, shifting my weight nervously on my feet. "So, about our plans tonight. Is there any way that we could reschedule? I completely hate to do it, but I had something come up that I can't get out of."

Noah offers me a small smile and yet again, there's nothing malicious that comes from him. "I already bought the tickets, but maybe I can see if I'm able to switch them to a different day."

"Crap," I mutter, hanging my head in defeat as the guilt overwhelms me. It doesn't come in waves. Instead, it's like a damn monsoon, completely consuming me in its depths. "I'm so sorry, Noah. It was something unexpected and I tried to get out of it."

"Would you care if I asked Eric or someone to go with me? We can do something else when we reschedule."

There's something about the way Noah speaks that has me realizing the exact thing I wondered about him. He's clearly oblivious, not even bothered by me needing to reschedule our plans. Either he's that understanding or he's what I thought. Flat. There's no depth, no layers. What you see is what you get.

And maybe that's not someone who I would want my future with, regardless of how safe he could be.

"Sure," I smile at him, nodding in agreement. "I

know how excited you were to go see this movie, so I would hate for you to miss it, especially when you already bought tickets. Would you want to do something another night this week that you might be free?"

Noah nods, smiling as he motions for me to walk in front of him into the classroom. "Of course," he says happily, following behind me as we step inside and find our seats. "I'm sure we can figure something else out to do. What about Thursday evening?"

"That sounds perfect," I tell him as we both sit down beside each other. "Thank you for being so understanding and flexible."

Noah smiles his perfect smile. "Of course, Olivia. Unexpected things come up all the time. That's the nature of life and I'm not going to be mad at you for it. Rescheduling is perfectly fine, as long as you still actually want to hang out."

The way he says the last few words has me filled with guilt again. "Of course, I want to hang out with you."

"Okay, good." He smiles, accepting my response. It's as if he believes anything I tell him without any hesitation or question. Not that he has any reason to think any differently of what I tell him, but it's just so unusual. There aren't many people like him. And that makes me want to keep him around even more.

People like Noah are hard to find. Ones who are genuine, not a single mean bone in their body. He's nice and I like him, but I'm not sure of my real feelings for him. He's attractive and literally the perfect person. I should be interested in him and I'm beginning to wonder if he might be interested in me, just with the way he made that last little comment.

He clearly wants to hang out with me and I feel bad for not choosing him.

Although, when it comes to Sterling, I'm not sure I would ever be able to fully choose someone over him. That's just the nature of the beast... of your first love and the hold they have on you.

———

It's just before six o'clock that I'm walking out of my building to wait for Sterling. He said he would be here, but I'm surprised when I see his deep blue car already sitting along the curb. The engine purrs and I wrap my coat tighter around my body as I walk over to where he's parked. I didn't see him at first, but I find him leaning against his car with his hands in the pockets of his coat.

His gaze lifts to mine and the corners of his lips tilt upwards as he pushes away from the passenger-side door. He's wearing jeans with black Vans. I'm not sure that I've seen him wear anything other than sweatpants or his suit that he has to wear to games. His gray hood hangs out over his black peacoat.

As I stop in front of him, I tilt my head back, his brown eyes shining back at me. His dark hair is a tousled mess, brushed away from his face. "Hey," I breathe, shifting my weight nervously in front of him. He wants to show me around town, but that doesn't mean anything.

Don't make it into something it's not, Olivia.

"Hey," Sterling repeats the word, sounding just as breathless. His cheeks are tinted with a pink hue, from the cold air that whips around us. "You ready to go?"

Yep," I respond as he turns around to open the car door for me. It's a small gesture, but it sends a warmth through me like I haven't felt in a long time. Sterling is usually cold, but I like this side of him. It's the version of Sterling I grew quite fond of when we were younger. It's the version I never see anymore. "Where are we going?"

Sterling shrugs with a smirk playing on his lips. I can't fight the grin that consumes my face as he slams the door shut. My eyes are on him, watching him walk around the front of the car before he comes to his side. It isn't often that Sterling smiles at anyone, unless it involves hockey.

I've missed this side of him more than words could ever describe.

He climbs into the driver's seat and I'm still watching him. His gaze collides with mine, lingering for a moment with something unreadable passing through his irises. His throat bobs as he swallows roughly, his eyes still shining brightly. Without a single word, he leans across the center console, the smell of him invading my senses.

He smells like the deep woods, the faint hints of cedar and pine, mixed with something sweet. Instinctively, I inhale deeply and my eyelids flutter shut. He's so close—*too close, really*—and I can't think straight. I don't know what he's doing until I hear the sound of a click.

Glancing down, I see that he was putting my seat belt on for me. Embarrassment instantly floods me, the heat creeping up my neck before spreading across my cheeks. As I lift my gaze back up, I see that he's still leaning over the center console. His face is just inches away from mine.

"Safety first, right?" There's a softness in his voice and I swear to God, I could melt.

My lips part slightly, a ragged breath slipping from my lips. His eyes drop down to my mouth and I watch as his tongue darts out, wetting his own lips. It's like a scene straight out of a movie. Sterling invading my space in his car. His gaze is glued to my mouth as he begins to lean closer.

Oh my god, he's going to kiss me.

He moves his hand from the buckle to the belt, pulling it a little tighter before he sits up straighter, moving away from me. His eyes meet mine in a rush, a fire burning deep within his irises as the corners of his lips lift slightly.

"We should get going before it gets late."

I'm a flustered mess, my face bright red as I tear my gaze away from his. He sits deeper in his seat, his hand finding the steering wheel as the other shifts the car into drive. And just like that, we're pulling away from the campus like that moment never happened.

And maybe to him it didn't.

CHAPTER TEN
STERLING

What the hell am I doing?

She's my little sister's best friend. She's always been completely off-limits. And if I wouldn't have just come to my senses, I definitely would have claimed her lips with my own. I like the effect I have on her; it feeds my ego, but in a different way than other girls ever have.

I never gave a shit about what they cared about. Impressing them wasn't something I was trying to do. It's not my fault they were always just drawn to me and we fell into arrangements like the one I had with Hannah. Olivia, on the other hand... her thoughts and opinions matter to me.

And knowing I have an effect on her gives me a boost of serotonin that gives me a rush. It's almost like a high. Olivia is an addiction and she's one that once she invades my bloodstream, I'll never be able to go without her.

"So, are you going to tell me where we're going?" Olivia questions me as we head toward the center of the city. She's been silently staring out the window, as if she's been trying to avoid me with being confined in such a small space with one another.

"I already told you," I tell her, looking at her from the corner of my eye. She isn't looking at me, but instead staring through the windshield. Snow begins to flurry from the dark night sky above us, landing on the glass before disappearing. "I want to show you around town."

"That doesn't really tell me much," she dead-pans, turning her head to me. I glance over, meeting her gaze briefly. "You can either just tell me now or prepare yourself for a million different questions."

A chuckle rumbles in my chest and I pull the car off to the side of the street. Bringing it to a stop along the curb, I put it in park and kill the engine before turning to look at her. "Can you do something for me tonight?"

"That depends."

"You can ask any questions except for what we're doing and where we're going." My lips lift in a grin as I give her the best puppy dog eyes I can muster. "Live life on the edge a little with me?"

Olivia sighs, her shoulders dropping in defeat. "How am I supposed to deny you when you're looking at me like that? I think I like the grumpy Sterling better. He's more of an asshole."

A laugh escapes me and Olivia looks at me like I have three heads. Licking my lips, I shrug at her. "Maybe you're rubbing off on me, sunshine."

Her lips part and she looks as if she's going to say something in response, but she doesn't. Instead she clamps them shut and I laugh to myself as I climb out of the car. As I walk around the front of it, Olivia is already getting out on her side. Her eyes are bright as they find mine and I step over to her, holding my arm out for her to slide hers through.

"What are you doing, Sterling?" she breathes, tentatively taking a step toward me as she slips her arm through mine.

The thought didn't fully cross my mind until now. *What am I doing?* There's no sense in dwelling over a small gesture like this and overthinking it. I'm just going to go with it—with her—tonight.

"Let's play a game," I murmur, catching the soft scent of her floral perfume.

Olivia tilts her head up to look at me. "What?"

"You're not Olivia tonight and I'm not Sterling," I tell her, knowing in the back of my mind that this is a terrible idea. Quite possibly the worst one I've ever had. I don't know where I'm going with this either. This is only going to end horribly.

"Then who are we?" she asks, her breath hitching.

The corners of my lips lift as I wink at her. "Whoever we want to be."

Olivia stares at me for a moment, her cheeks a rose tint from the cold air. My heart is in my throat as I wait for her response. Part of me is beginning to even regret suggesting such a thing.

"Okay," she smiles, taking me by surprise. There's a look of mischief in her eyes and it's foreign. Olivia always plays it safe, but not tonight. Tonight, she wants to play. "Can we get some food, though? Because I am starving."

"That's our first stop," I tell her, my legs moving as I pull her along with me.

There's a crêperie at the corner of the block. In the past three years that I've been at Wyncote, I've never been here once. But I remember when we were younger that Olivia always loved crêpes. She and Stella used to have me take them to one back in our hometown all the time. And even when I stopped taking them, they still went there together.

It's Olivia's favorite food and I want tonight to be special for her.

As we reach the end of the block, I lead Olivia to the front door, releasing her arm as I pull it open. The aroma of pastries floats out around us and Olivia looks up at me with a huge grin on her face as I hold open the door for her.

"You remembered," she says softly, her voice filled with emotion. She catches me off guard with the way she's looking at me like *I'm* the sun. But she's got it all wrong... I'm just merely a cloud hanging in her sky.

"I'll always remember."

Olivia stares at me for a moment, her face almost looking as if she's seen a ghost as the smile falls from her lips. Something unreadable passes through her expression before she recovers and heads inside. I follow after her, feeling a little off as we walk up to the counter.

After looking at the menu and ordering our food, we find a table tucked away in the corner. Olivia is quieter than normal as we wait for someone to bring out our food. Her questions are superficial and her smile is fake. I know the look on her face right now.

It's the mask she wears for everyone. It's not the smile she has reserved just for me.

The one that feels like a tornado tearing through my chest.

I answer her questions, and most of them seem to be about hockey. I'm not here to talk about any of that with her, but I play along. If I want her to play my game tonight, I need to let her lead right now until she's feeling comfortable again. I'm just not sure what made her feel uncomfortable in the first place.

After we finish eating, we both bundle back up and put on our coats before stepping out into the frigid night. As we walk down the street, it feels as though the distance between us is growing. Her arm isn't in mine like when we first got here and I find myself missing her warmth. I want her floral scent surrounding me, invading my senses until I can't think straight.

Taking a chance, I sidestep, moving closer to her. Her arm hangs down by her side and I slip my hand into hers. Olivia half stops, glancing up at me with her eyes wide. I don't know what the hell I'm doing. I'm crossing a line that I swore to myself I would never cross. This was a place I never wanted to go because I knew what giving in to that temptation would do.

"Sterling," she murmurs my name softly, the sound like velvet as it slides across my eardrums.

"No, babe," I say quietly, my eyes finding hers as snow flurries begin to fall around us. "Remember, we're whoever we want to be tonight. Don't over-think any of this. Just live on the edge with me."

She stops completely and I halt alongside her. Her warm palm is still pressed against mine, our fingers laced together. "What happens if I fall?"

Fuck.

My throat constricts and I swallow roughly over the lump lodged inside. Her eyes desperately search mine as my heart pounds erratically in my chest.

"Then I'll be the one to catch you."

CHAPTER ELEVEN
OLIVIA

My eyes widen as I stare back at Sterling. I know I shouldn't be doing this. There's no way this could possibly end well. I know how he operates and the way he goes through girls as if it's nothing. He doesn't form attachments with any of them. It's always no strings attached. If there's one person that can turn my world upside down, while shredding my heart at the same time, it's Sterling Barrett.

And he's standing here staring at me like he's ready to show me the world. Before he rips the rug out from under my feet and I'm forced to face reality. I'm no different than any of the other girls. In fact, I'm probably far worse. Completely off-limits because of being best friends with his sister. There's no way that Stella would ever approve of me doing anything with her brother. Hell, if she were here right now, she'd probably lose her shit with us holding hands.

"What's going on in that beautiful head of yours?" Sterling questions me, turning to face me. I follow suit, the toes of our shoes touching as he continues to hold my hand. He moves his thumb back and forth, slowly stroking my cold skin.

"What about Hannah?"

I can't stop the question as it's falling from my lips. My mind wanders back to their interaction at the diner. It's clear that there was something going on between them. I'm still in the dark about the details of their relationship. And I'm not about to be the one who gets involved with someone who is already taken.

Then again, I'm also kind of seeing Noah. Maybe not officially, but we've been spending a lot of time together. He's kind and soft. He's the opposite of Sterling. He's the safer option. If I get involved with Sterling, then that all goes away.

Sterling's eyebrows tug together as he tilts his head to the side. "What about her?"

"Aren't the two of you together or something?"

Sterling chuckles, lifting his other hand as he

brushes a piece of hair away from my face. His fingertips are soft against my skin as he tucks the lock behind my ear. "No. We were fucking around, but that was it. Plus, I ended that shit after that night at the diner."

His words hit me deep in the chest. "You didn't go see her even though you made plans with her?"

"Nah." Sterling shakes his head, his fingers trailing down the side of my face and along my jawline. "I blew her off because I couldn't get this other girl out of my head. It didn't feel like the right thing to do."

My heart hammers harder in my chest and it feels like it could burst through my rib cage at any given moment. The butterflies in my stomach flutter as a rush of euphoria courses through my veins.

"I don't think you're thinking clearly," I whisper, not fully trusting my voice.

Sterling stares at me for a moment as he cups the side of my face. "I feel the opposite—like I'm finally seeing things clearly. Can I tell you a secret?" he asks me as his face dips down to mine. "I've always seen you, Olivia. You've always invaded my thoughts, but you've always been off-limits."

"What changes things now?"

His lips lift upward into a grin. "I'm tired of

playing things safe. What's life if you're not taking risks?"

"I like safe," I whisper.

"Then let me be your safety net," Sterling breathes before claiming my mouth with his own. His lips are soft and warm against mine. We're lost in the moment and I let him sweep me away. Moving my lips with his, he slides his tongue along the seam. I let him in, his tongue moving against mine.

He tastes like strawberries and whip cream. I've always imagined what it would be like kissing him and this completely exceeds my expectations. He's skilled, where I'm much more inexperienced. He kisses me like I've never been kissed before. Our tongues are caught in a dance to their own melody as he steals the air from my lungs.

My head swims, my heart pounding erratically in my chest. It's cold outside, standing in the night as snow flurries swirl around us. But he warms me from the inside out. This is the old Sterling I grew to love and he's finally let me in—the one place I always craved to be.

He pulls away, leaving me completely breathless as he leans his forehead against mine. "I'm sorry I've always been an asshole to you. It made it easier to resist you, to pretend that there was nothing there."

My chest heaves with every shallow breath I take. My heart is going wild in its cage, but I feel safe with Sterling's hand cupping the side of my face. "I don't know what we're doing here, Sterling."

"We're living, babe," he breathes, lifting his head as he presses his lips to my forehead. "Don't over-think any of it. Just live in the moment with me."

"What happens after this moment ends?"

"What if it never has to?" he counters.

I swallow roughly over the emotion that wells in my throat. "I've been hanging out with someone else and I'm afraid that he has feelings for me."

"Do you have feelings for him?" Sterling asks me, pulling back as his eyes desperately search mine. A shadow passes over his expression as a wave of panic passes through his irises.

I shake my head. "I don't think so. I wanted to because he's safe and nice..." I pause for a moment and choose honesty over lying to him. "But he isn't you."

"Get rid of him," Sterling says, his voice low and his tone cold. "I'm right here, Olivia. I'm showing all of my cards that I've been playing close to my chest for fucking years."

"It's not that easy," I tell him, frowning. "We're friends and I don't want to ruin that."

Sterling stares at me for a moment and I swear, it's like he's staring directly into my soul. Although, there's a darkness in his eyes that I can't quite put into words. I don't like it, the way it sends a shiver down my spine.

"Okay," he says quietly, nodding thoughtfully. I still don't like the look in his eyes, almost as if he doesn't really agree with it, but I don't question him on it. "Let's not talk about any of that shit and just enjoy the rest of the night."

"What happens after tonight, though?" I question him, unable to keep the thought to myself. I need to know his answer because this moment isn't what scares me. It's the future and the unknown. We're alone right now, and this is how he was when we were younger and no one else was around.

How am I to know that it won't be the way it was before when we're around other people?

"That's up to you, babe," Sterling says, his hand still in mine as he turns away from me and begins to walk down the sidewalk. I follow along with him, falling into step beside him. "Take your time and do whatever you need to do. I'm not going anywhere."

My heart clenches. There's something in his tone

that makes me wonder if there are words he's leaving out. He says he isn't going anywhere, but what does that even mean? There's too much to think about and he's clouding my mind right now. I'm not thinking straight with him near me like this.

"Get out of your head, Liv," he says softly as he gently squeezes my hand. "Be here with me right now and we'll worry about the rest tomorrow."

Will we really, though?

I don't know if I can believe what he's saying. He can't guarantee me anything, but he only asked me for one thing tonight. To live life on the edge with him. That we can be anyone we want to be.

So, for tonight, I'm going to enjoy this time with him as whoever he wants me to be.

And then all I can do is hope that things don't change when tomorrow comes.

CHAPTER TWELVE
STERLING

As I roll over in bed the next morning, the night before plays over in my head. After we kissed on the sidewalk, I took Olivia to two different art galleries. One of them was displaying my teammate's fiancé's work in there. Logan was so proud of Isla so when he heard that I was going to be in the area, he asked me to stop and check it out to show support.

Olivia thought it was the coolest thing, that I knew one of the artists personally. She hasn't met either of them, but I fully intend on introducing them all. I know Olivia has her reservations, that she doesn't think I was serious last night, but she was wrong.

I kissed her again last night in the gardens and

then once more when I dropped her back off at her dorm. As badly as I wanted to take her back to my house and have her in my bed, it wasn't an option. I've already crossed too many lines and completely blurred any others that were drawn.

Then again, lines were meant to be crossed and erased. I don't feel an ounce of guilt for finally being honest with Olivia and myself. It felt freeing, to finally admit my feelings for her and letting myself actually feel them.

I know she probably spent the rest of the night questioning every moment between us. Even though I told her I wasn't going anywhere, she didn't fully believe me. How could she? Everything that I admitted to her was a stark contrast to how I've treated her over the years. The cold persona I put on, the mask of being an asshole. None of that mattered because it wasn't the truth.

The truth is, I've always seen Olivia and I'm tired of fucking ignoring it. Fuck my sister, fuck anyone who has a problem with it. I won't stop until I make her mine, now.

There's just one obstacle that keeps poking me in the side like a thorn. That fucking asshole she's been hanging out with. He's got to go... and if Olivia doesn't do something about him, I will.

Reaching over on my nightstand, I grab my phone and roll onto my back. Holding it above my face, I unlock the screen and open my messages app. I find the thread with Olivia from the first night Stella called me about her and I open it up. Rereading over them, my stomach sinks. I really was an asshole to her.

I want to delete all of the messages I sent to her that day, but I leave them instead. Fuck it. It's a reminder of how I don't want to act toward her again. Instead, I'll just show her I'm not the same guy I was before. That wasn't the real me and I was just hiding from the growing feelings I had for her—the ones I buried deep inside.

STERLING

Good morning, sunshine.

Not giving myself a chance to second-guess it, I send her the text. It isn't much, but it's a way to break through to start a conversation with her. That's all I need. Something to splinter the ice between us. And after she lets me in, then I'll fucking shatter it all.

I set my phone back on my nightstand before finally climbing out of bed. I have a few classes this morning and then that's it for the day. Although, we have a practice this evening and then a game tomorrow night. So, I can't slack on my responsibilities entirely. As badly as I want to say fuck my classes, I can't do that either.

I'm so close to graduation, so close to reaching the finish line. I don't have plans of doing anything with my degree since I'm after the NHL dream like the rest of the guys. I have to have the degree as a backup plan, though, in case my dreams don't come true. There's always that chance and that's the risk that you have to be willing to take if you're going to shoot past the stars.

I have no intention of giving up on that dream. And in order to keep the wheels turning with the plans I have, I need to maintain my grades. Skipping any classes while being this close to graduation isn't the best thing I could be doing. This is me trying to be the responsible Sterling.

My phone vibrates on the nightstand as I walk over to my closet and grab a change of clothes. Holding them in my arm, I grab my phone and head out of my room as I read Olivia's message.

OLIVIA

Good morning :)

A smile pulls on my lips as I step into the bathroom and put my stuff down on the counter. I turn on the shower quickly before typing a message back to Olivia.

STERLING

How did you sleep?

I set my phone down on the counter, stripping out of my clothes. It doesn't take long for Olivia to respond and I grab my phone, reading over her message as I stand naked in the bathroom.

OLIVIA

I slept really well, thanks. How about you?

Without thinking, I type the first thing that comes to my mind. I've already told her more than I ever intended on revealing, so fuck it. There's no sense in playing it safe now. I'm going all in because there's no other option. There's no going back and I have no intention of doing that.

STERLING

I would have slept better if you would have been in my bed with me.

I watch as it changes from delivered to read

underneath my message. Three small bubbles pop up in the bottom left corner and quickly disappear. Smirking at my phone, I watch them reappear and disappear three different times before I lock my screen and set my phone down on the counter.

I think it's safe to say I left her speechless. Or at least without some sunshine response that she would usually have. Olivia isn't used to this side of me, but she's about to be. I've talked dirty with other girls before, but not like this. Not through messages and ones with different meanings. The things I've said to other girls were never on a level this personal.

I'd be stupid to not want Olivia in my bed. But that doesn't mean it's just sexual with her. I mean, we've only kissed a few times and that just happened last night. There hasn't been anything sexual even though I intend on that happening eventually. I just hope this doesn't scare her away.

And if it does, I have no problem chasing after her.

I've never chased after a girl before, but Olivia is one I would travel across the world to hunt down. I pushed her away before in the past to try and keep both of us safe, but not anymore. I'm not letting her go ever again.

Hopping into the shower, my dick is already hard as thoughts of Olivia drift into my mind. If she would have come home with me last night, she would be in here with me right now, no doubt about it. The thought of her standing in the water, completely naked as it trails down her body. I'd lick every drop of water from her skin. Fuck, I'd lick every inch of her goddamn flesh.

Ignoring my raging hard-on, I fight the urge to jerk off to the thought of her again. I take the quickest shower in the history of showers before hopping back out. My body is completely clean, washed, and dried in record time. Wrapping my towel around my waist, I check my phone and my heart pounds in my chest as I see Olivia sent me a text back.

OLIVIA

Why didn't you invite me back to your place then?

Holy fuck.

I didn't expect her to take the bait and play along, but I completely underestimated her. Perhaps Olivia isn't as cautious and safe as I always chalked her up to be. Maybe there's something dark and dirty hiding deep inside of her. She can be my little freak, but no one else's. The thought of her talking like this to someone else has my blood boiling, but that doesn't matter.

What matters right now is the fact that she's waiting for a response. And I fully intend on giving her what she wants.

STERLING

Would you have come with me if I asked you?

OLIVIA

Yes… but you didn't ask.

STERLING

Because I didn't want to push things too far too fast. Fuck, baby. I just got out of the shower and I wish you were here with me.

I regret sending that message as soon as I do. I literally just contradicted myself in two sentences. I started it off saying I didn't want to push things, but then openly admitted that I wish she were here with me right now.

Fucking idiot.

OLIVIA

What would you do to me if I were there with you right now?

Holy fucking shit, what is happening?

My cock throbs, still hard as a rock as it presses through my towel. It's only eight o'clock in the morning and I have Olivia sexting me right now. Never in my wildest dreams did I ever think that this would be my reality. And I plan on taking full advantage of it.

STERLING

I'd drop to my knees and eat your pussy while you're wet in the shower. And then after you come on my tongue, I'd bend you over and fuck you from behind.

Was that too forward? Probably. But she asked and I'm only giving her the truth from now on. If she doesn't like it, I won't come on to her like this anymore until she's ready. I don't know how experienced she is, so that's a conversation we definitely need to have sometime.

OLIVIA

Is that it?

Fuck. This girl is driving me mad right now.

Lifting my palm to my mouth, I spit in it before dropping my hand down to my cock. I push away my towel and wrap my hand around myself, stroking my length as I picture Olivia right now.

STERLING

Oh no, baby. We'd just be getting started.

I imagine her laying in her dorm room right now, spread out on her bed as her fingers slide in and out of her tight pussy. She's pressing on her clit, rolling her thumb around in circles as she continues to finger fuck herself to my messages. To the thoughts of my cock balls deep inside of her.

STERLING

Touch yourself, baby. You've got me as hard as a rock right now.

OLIVIA

I will if you will.

Jesus goddamn Christ.

STERLING

Already am.

I pull on my cock, my hand pumping faster as my hips begin to buck. I fuck my hand, imagining that it's Olivia instead. Closing my eyes, I see her as she continues to pleasure herself with thoughts of me instead.

My balls constrict, drawing closer to my body as I reach the top of the cliff. I can't help it as my orgasm hits me like a fucking tidal wave. I was trying to hold out, but the longer I stroke my cock and think about Olivia, there's no way I can hold this in anymore. Jesus Christ, what I wouldn't give to be in her bed right now. With me inside of her instead of her fingers pumping in and out of that pretty pussy.

A groan slips from my lips, vibrating in my chest, as I let out a ragged breath. Warmth spreads through my body as I'm overcome with the euphoric state from my release. My cum is all over my hand with some dripping down onto my towel on the floor.

I stare down at my phone, my lips parted as my chest heaves with every breath I take. It's like coming up for fresh air but I still can't breathe. I need more of her to feed my body, like oxygen. This was a nice, unexpected little treat with her, but it isn't enough. I'm fucking greedy and I want more.

Fuck the rest. At this point, nothing else matters in my mind except getting closer to Olivia. I should be worried about the consequences of my actions, but I'm not. I should be worried about the future because I know that I can't give her the future she deserves, but I'm not worried about that either.

The only thing that matters to me is this moment and what I can do in it.

And the one thing I can think of is making Olivia mine.

Not in the sense of her being my girlfriend. I don't do commitments because they only turn into obligations and that's one thing I won't subject Olivia to. She deserves more than I will ever be able to give her. Plus, she's a freshman; I'm a senior. After I graduate, I'm out of here. If I can get drafted into the NHL, I'm going to whatever team will take me.

Call me selfish or greedy, but it is what it is.

I will get Olivia Davis in my bed before this semester is over.

CHAPTER THIRTEEN
OLIVIA

As I'm walking to class, I can't help but feel like everyone knows. Heat creeps up my neck, spreading across my cheeks as I pass other classmates in the hall. I avoid any eye contact possible, keeping my gaze trained on the ground below my feet.

What happened with Sterling this morning was something I've never done before. I'm as unexperienced as they come. I had a boyfriend in high school, but I didn't ever have sex with him. It's like in my mind, I subconsciously knew that he wasn't important enough to me. He didn't deserve that part of me. So, every time we got close to it happening, I pulled away from him.

He never protested, but I think it's because he

half expected for me to come to my senses and for it to happen eventually. But it never did. Now, I'm in college with little experience and my hymen still intact. This morning was the first time I ever did something like that with someone over the phone.

And I can't believe I did it with Sterling freaking Barrett.

Of all people for me to get involved with like that, it just had to be him. It's something I've wanted to happen since we were kids and I developed an unhealthy crush for him. I just never thought my dream would ever be within my reach.

I know Sterling well enough to know it doesn't mean anything to him in the grand scheme of things. If you aren't a stick or a puck, you don't matter in the long run. I've seen him go through so many different girls over the years, none of them ever stuck. And it wasn't because they didn't want to be around. It's because Sterling always kicked them to the curb without a second thought about it.

I don't know what his real issue was. It was almost as if he didn't think he deserved to have it all. Having a girl and still being able to play hockey was just not a possibility in his mind. Doesn't he realize that people make sacrifices and make things work?

Or maybe he was just like the way I was with

Ben and my virginity... None of the girls that Sterling ever dated or slept with were deserving of his heart.

I continue to walk, counting my steps as the classroom that I need is at the end of this hall. My mind is somewhere else completely and I don't even notice that someone is standing in front of me until I'm colliding into a solid, warm chest.

A gasp slips from my lips and I inhale deeply as I lift my head, meeting his eyes. His scent invades my senses and I feel my heart crawl into my chest as I stare up at Sterling. There's a ghost of a smirk on his lips, because God forbid he ever lets a smile consume his expression.

"I was hoping I would run into you," he says softly, a chuckle vibrating in his chest after his words. "I was wondering if we would run into each other like this again."

I swallow hard, shifting my weight nervously as I smile up at him. "Sorry about that. I wasn't paying attention and was a little distracted."

Sterling tilts his head to the side, raising an eyebrow at me. "Oh yeah? What has you so distracted right now?" I don't miss the lilt in his voice and I know exactly what he's implying.

And damn him for hitting the nail on the head.

"Um, you know... just stuff."

"Right," he chuckles, his eyes shining brightly at me. "Let me walk you to class?"

My eyes widen slightly as his question catches me off guard. "You don't have to do that," I tell him, my voice quiet as I glance around the hall. I'm sure he's offering just to be nice, but then again, Sterling isn't usually nice like this. "I'm just at the end of the hallway here, so it's really okay."

"I know, Olivia," his voice is hoarse as he stares directly through me. "I don't have to, but I want to."

"Oh," I respond, my breath catching in my throat. "Okay."

We both turn simultaneously and fall in step beside one another as we head in the direction of the classroom. I don't think that Sterling has a class anywhere near mine this morning, so there's no reason for him to be over here right now. Unless he actually did walk over here just to see me. Which, in that case, he's going to be late for his own class.

As we walk in silence down the hall, I see Noah standing outside the door waiting for me. He's predictable and doesn't do anything that would ever cause any surprise. He waits for me every morning, so there's no reason to expect anything different from him.

"What are you doing tonight?" Sterling questions me, not noticing Noah outside the door.

"Nothing," I tell him honestly. "I was probably going to study or something. Or just read. I don't really ever have any plans."

"Come study with me," he offers, turning his head to look down at me. "When is your last class? I'll pick you up afterward."

I push away the nervousness that wells inside of me. "I'll be done around four-thirty."

We reach the doorway to the classroom and Sterling's jaw clenches as his eyes drift over to Noah, who offers me a wave. I wave back at him, smiling brightly before looking back at Sterling. A shadow passes through his expression, his eyes growing dark as he stares back at me. A shiver trails up my spine as his cold gaze is glued to mine.

I don't know what to expect, bracing myself for him to just walk away or give me some kind of attitude. Instead, he steps closer into my space, his fingertips brushing against my face as he pushes a stray lock of hair behind my ear.

My breath is caught in my throat as he closes the distance between us, his head right beside mine and his hand still cupping the side of my face. His breath is warm against my ear and his lips are soft as they skate across my skin.

"Get rid of him, Olivia," he murmurs as he nips at the bottom lobe of my ear. I'm still holding my breath, waiting for him to say something else as a warmth floods my body. This is the effect he has on me and sometimes I can't help but hate it.

Instead of offering any more words, Sterling pulls away from me, cold replacing his warmth against my face. Without another word, he turns his back to me and strides away, disappearing in a crowd of students as he makes his way toward the stairs.

Letting out the breath I was holding, I walk over to Noah, my smile not quite reaching my eyes as I meet up with him. His eyebrows are drawn together, but there's nothing malicious in his expression. Just curiosity instead.

"Who was that?" he questions me as he pulls open the door and holds it for me to step through.

Swallowing roughly, I shake my head dismissively. "Just a friend. He was walking me to class."

"It looked like it was a little more than that, Olivia," he says, his voice filled with concern. "Sterling, right? He doesn't seem like the most pleasant person."

"He isn't," I agree with a shrug as we find our seats in the classroom. "But sometimes he can be nice."

"Just be careful with him," Noah warns quietly. I look up at him, meeting his concerned eyes. "Guys like him are nothing but trouble."

I force a smile to my lips as I nod at Noah. "I appreciate your concern, but he's just a friend. I've known him my entire life so I know what to expect with Sterling."

"So, there's nothing going on between the two of you then?" Noah asks, his voice soft and gentle, just like his soul.

I shake my head, not sure how to respond. I don't know what the hell is actually going on between us, but I'm not going to be the first person to admit that there is more than what I'm telling Noah. "He's just a friend."

"Good," Noah sighs in relief, a smile tugging on the corners of his lips. "Because I really like you, Olivia. And if I'm going to have some kind of competition, I'd like to know what I'm up against."

The air leaves my lungs in a defeated sigh as I sink down into my seat. I like Noah, but he isn't Sterling. He's nice and he's safe. I've grown relatively close to him in the short amount of time we've been friends. He's quite literally the only friend I have and while I've given the thought of something more with him, I don't know if that's a line I would ever cross.

And now Sterling is involved. He's in my head and under my skin. He wants me to erase Noah from the equation, but I don't know if I'm ready to. He's the safer option between the two. It's not fair to string him along when I have feelings for someone else, but I don't know if I'm ready to close the page to that chapter yet.

At some point, I'm going to have to let him go. I'm going to have to end whatever this is before it progresses to something more.

How the hell am I going to let him down without ruining our friendship in the process?

CHAPTER FOURTEEN
STERLING

I'm waiting for Olivia in the parking lot at the time she said she would be done with her last class. I should have given her some time to go back to her room if she wanted to, but I don't know if I can wait any longer to see her. I don't know what my issue is—why the hell I feel so goddamn obsessed with this girl right now.

There hasn't been another girl that has occupied my mind the way Olivia does. Maybe it's because I've known her for so long, I know her better than I've ever known anyone else.

Either way, I don't like the way she clouds my thoughts.

So, here I am, waiting to take her back to my place and hopefully fuck her out of my system.

That's an exaggeration. As badly as I want her in my bed, I have no intention of fucking her today. But I will be fucking her one of these days, as long as she's on board with the idea.

And judging from our texts this morning, I'd be willing to bet my left nut that she wants it just as much as I do.

Olivia breaks through a crowd of people that are near the doorway as she pauses outside the door. Her head turns, her eyes scanning the parking lot, when she sees me parked alongside the curb. Her footsteps are light and she moves quickly through the frigid winter air as she heads over to me. Leaning over the center console, I pull the handle and push open the door for her.

I see that asshole friend of hers lingering in the background, watching the two of us from a distance with a frown on his face. I can't fight the smile that pulls on my lips as I see the disappointment in his expression.

That's right, motherfucker.

Olivia Davis is mine, not yours.

"Hey," I say softly as she climbs into the car and straps on her seat belt. "How was the rest of your day?"

"Good," Olivia smiles at me, sitting deeper in her seat. "How was yours?"

I smile at her. "It's much better now."

I watch the pink tint creep across her cheeks and she shifts her weight in her seat. I love the effect I have on her, the way I can make her squirm just from being around her. My gaze is heated on hers and I want her to climb across the center console and sit herself on my lap.

Jesus Christ, what is wrong with me?

My cock is half hard in my pants and now I'm the one adjusting my weight in an attempt to hide it. Olivia fucking ruined me and I haven't even felt her skin under my fingertips yet.

"Are you okay?" Olivia asks me quietly as my knuckles turn white from how tightly I'm gripping the steering wheel. I glance over at her, putting one hand on the stick as I offer her a small smile.

"Just great," I lie, not wanting to fully conceal my feelings right now. Feelings are one thing that I've always been against, yet I can't help the way that my heart pounds harder when Olivia is near me.

Putting the car in drive, I pull away from the curb and head out of the parking lot. Olivia begins to talk—

or ramble—about her day. I notice the way she's about to say his name but she quickly diverts the conversation elsewhere. I know she didn't tell him to back off with the way he was watching us from campus today.

It would be nicer of Olivia if she would be the one to tell him to get lost. I have a feeling it's not going to be that simple, though. She's too nice to let anyone down. And if she doesn't do it soon, I'm going to be left with no choice but to take matters into my own hands, because I refuse to share her with anyone else.

We finally pull up to my house and I silently thank the guys for not being here. I don't want Olivia around them—not yet. Not until I figure out what her feelings really are and what her true thoughts are on all of this. I have a proposition for her, but I want to make sure she agrees before I bring her into my world.

Olivia follows me into the house and it feels strange. She's the first girl I've ever brought home. Anyone else I've fucked around with, I always went to their place or in their car or anywhere other than my own house or vehicle.

But I want Olivia in my space. I want her consuming every goddamn inch.

Her gaze is gentle as she looks around the living

room area, following me into the modern style kitchen as I pause by the fridge. I pull it open, grabbing two waters while Olivia patiently waits. She's a goddamn saint. I don't know that there's a single flaw in this girl, besides the way she approaches everything with caution. But then again, that might not be a flaw at all.

"Do you want to go up to my room to study?"

Olivia looks at me for a moment, an unreadable look in her eyes as she slowly nods her head. "Sure. You have other roommates, right?"

Reaching for the strap of her backpack, I remove it from her shoulder and sling it over my own. "I do, but neither of them should be home until later tonight. If you want to study down here instead, we can do that."

Olivia shakes her head, her throat bobbing as she swallows roughly. "No, your room is fine."

My throat feels like it's coated with peanut butter and I clear it before turning to walk back through the house. Olivia follows after me and we make our way upstairs and into the hall. My room is down at the other end and Olivia's footsteps are light as she walks behind me.

We step into my bedroom and she stands in the center for a moment, looking around at my space.

There isn't much to it. A bed, a dresser with a TV, and I have a small desk in the corner. The only things that decorate my room are hockey memorabilia.

Olivia turns to look at me, a smile on her face as I set her bag down on the floor. "Your room looks exactly like your childhood bedroom did."

Tilting my head to the side, I narrow my eyes slightly. "What does that mean?"

The lilt of her laughter hits my eardrums and it sounds like a melody I could get lost in. "It's the exact same. The only thing you have is hockey-related stuff."

I stare at her for a moment, missing the joke. "Would you expect anything else? Hockey is the only thing that matters."

Her face falls for a moment and I don't miss the pained look that washes through her irises before she recovers. She smiles at me and nods. "I know, Sterling. I just thought it was amusing that it's really no different than your old room."

I instantly feel regret for being a bit of an asshole about it. She wasn't trying to make a joke, just making an observation. One that she found amusing, and I kind of took the amusement right out of it by being an asshole. I don't know what made her recoil the way it did, but I still feel guilty for it.

"What do you have to study for?" I ask her as I drop down onto my bed and pull her backpack up with me. "Maybe it's a class I've already taken that I could help you with?"

Olivia sits down beside me, a smile on her face as she kicks off her shoes and tucks her legs underneath her like this is exactly where she belongs. She confused me with the way she acts like she doesn't know how to talk or walk right around me but then at the same time will act like she's more comfortable with me than she's ever been with anyone else.

I don't know what to make of Olivia Davis anymore. She's more complex than I had ever realized.

She laughs lightly, shrugging off her coat. "I highly doubt that," she responds as I take her coat from her and go hang it over the back of the chair by my desk. "It's for one of my biology classes and I would be willing to bet that you only took the required classes you had to."

"Okay, okay." I throw my hands up in defeat as I walk over to her and drop back down onto the bed. "You got me there. You know that I'm definitely not here for a biology degree so I only took whatever science classes I had to take. And with marketing, there aren't many science classes needed for that degree."

"That's what you decided to major in?" she questions me, tilting her head to the side with a thoughtful look in her eye. "That's an unexpected one."

I shrug. "I mean, you know that hockey is the endgame for where I'm planning on my career going, but it seemed like a decent one for a backup career. That way if anything happens, I can always get involved in some type of sports marketing or something like that."

"Would you really accept anything other than playing professionally? That's been your lifelong dream, Sterling. You never struck me as the type of person to let anything get in your way of achieving your dreams."

I smile at her, feeling like someone can actually fucking see me. That's one thing I love about Olivia. All of the other girls liked me for my status on the hockey team. They wanted to be involved with an athlete that was semi-popular. And then if I make it pro, they could use me as clout. But not Olivia. She doesn't give a shit about any of that.

The only thing she's worried about is me actually achieving the dreams and goals that I have. Not what she can benefit from.

"So, did you want to study or just watch a movie or something instead?"

Olivia grabs her books, pulling one onto her lap as she flips it open. "I do have one assignment I have to finish that is due tomorrow. You can busy yourself while I finish it and then we can watch a movie?"

"Yes, ma'am." I wink at her, lying back on my bed. "I'm just going to study the insides of my eyelids until you're ready."

Olivia rolls her eyes. "You don't have to worry about any of your classes, do you?"

"I'm graduating this year, babe," I tell her, a smirk tugging on the corners of my lips. Yet again, the word slipped, but I'm just going to keep moving like I don't even notice. Olivia noticed and I can tell by the way her eyes widen. "All of my grades are exactly where I need them to be, so I'm not worrying about that shit if I don't have to."

She nods, something unreadable in her expression before she drops her attention back to her book. Bending my elbows, I slide my hands under the back of my head and close my eyes to give her some time to do whatever it is she needs to do. I can't help myself as I find my eyes opening every few minutes to look at her.

I might not have anything to do for any of my classes, but I want to study too...

Study her.

She's quite literally the most beautiful sight I have ever seen. I love the way her perfectly straight nose crinkles when she reads something she doesn't quite understand. Her eyebrows draw together, before her face relaxes. She's the fucking sun that hangs in the sky above, shining through the darkest clouds on the darkest of days.

After about an hour of us sitting in silence, Olivia finally closes her book and tucks it back into her backpack before sliding it onto the ground. She turns to look at me as I sit back up in my bed, my eyes searching hers.

"Are you all done?" I ask her, my voice soft and thick with emotion after just studying her for the past hour.

She nods, a small smile on her eyes. "You said you wanted to watch a movie. What did you have in mind?"

I shrug. "I don't know, I don't know what is new or good. Did you have any ideas?"

Olivia laughs lightly and that goddamn sound

hits me directly in the center of my chest. My heart constricts and I find myself inching closer to her on the bed. "Are you okay with emotional movies? I know you probably don't like sappy shit, but I kind of do."

"I like whatever you like."

Leaning across the bed, she grabs the remote from me, a smirk on her face. My skin tingles from where her fingers brush across mine. I want to burn in her fucking fire. I watch Olivia as she pulls away and flicks on the TV, scrolling until she stops on a movie.

"*Five Feet Apart*?" I ask her, my eyebrows tugging together.

"Shh," she lifts her finger to her lips, "don't knock it until you actually watch it."

A smile tugs on my lips and Olivia scoots up to the headboard beside me. We're side by side in my bed, both of our eyes glued to the TV as the movie begins. It's killing me being this close to her right now, but in a sense, I'm completely comfortable.

Although, I don't know if I can keep my hands to myself if we lay here after the movie is over.

CHAPTER FIFTEEN
OLIVIA

I'm a sobbing mess by the time the movie is over. Turning my head, I look over at Sterling, who is watching me with his eyes wet. No tears fall from them but I can see the way he's holding back. There's something unreadable in his expression, like there are words on the tip of his tongue and he doesn't know how to articulate them.

A forced laugh falls from my lips and I shake my head, suddenly embarrassed as I swipe the tears away from my face. "I'm sorry," I laugh, smiling at Sterling. "This movie gets me every freaking time."

Sterling's throat bobs as he swallows roughly. A fire burns in his eyes as they're filled with emotion. "Don't," he murmurs, wrapping his hand around my wrist as he pulls my hand away from my face.

"Leave the tears. You look beautiful with or without them."

He steals the oxygen from the room and my wrist burns under his touch as I get lost in the fire burning in his eyes. Time is suspended in the air and I suddenly can't form any words. It isn't often that I'm rendered speechless, but Sterling has me caught right now.

And I'm afraid I don't want him to ever let me go.

"Olivia," he says quietly, his voice thick with emotion. "I don't know what it is about you, but I can't get you out of my goddamn head. You're always there, creeping around in the darkest corners. No matter what I try to do, I can't seem to get you out of my system. You're under my skin, burrowing yourself deeper and deeper each and every fucking moment."

My lips part slightly and I stare back at him, my eyes bouncing back and forth between his rapidly. If I wasn't speechless before, I'm at a complete loss for words right now. After the other night when Sterling took me out, he surprised me then with things that I never thought were real.

But now, here we are in his bed and he's laying it all out for me. We aren't pretending to be whoever we want tonight. We're just Olivia and Sterling. And he's giving me more than he ever has before.

"Sterling…" I start softly, my voice trailing off as I don't know what I should say to him. I know what I want to say to him—the exact things I've been keeping to myself for years. But I can't do that. If I do that, I'm only asking him to break my heart… which might not be such a bad thing anymore.

I would rather have him break my heart than to never get to experience his love.

"I don't want you to fall in love with him, Olivia," Sterling admits, his voice cracking around his words. "Fall in love with me instead."

He literally steals all of the oxygen from the room, leaving me completely breathless. First he said he wanted to be one of my safety nets and now he wants me to fall in love with him. What happened to being off-limits? There are so many variables when it comes to this—so many what-ifs.

I've spent most of my life being cautious and living it on the safe side. I can't help but be nervous as all the millions of tragic possibilities flood my brain. And they all lead back to getting my heart broken.

"What about Stella?" I ask him, my voice barely

audible as I don't fully trust it myself. "She would never approve."

A chuckle vibrates in Sterling's chest. "You know my sister better than that. She might be a little annoyed at first, but I don't know that she would really give a shit."

"Can I be honest with you for a second?" I ask him, not wanting to go here, but he brought this whole thing on. I don't know how else to approach it.

"Of course," he says gently. "I don't want you to ever feel like you can't be honest with me. You don't have to tell me what you think I want to hear."

"I don't want to get involved with you because of the future. You have plans and goals of greatness after you graduate. I'm still a freshman. It would never work because of the uncertainty about the future."

Sterling stares at me for a moment and he's silent as he tilts his head to the side. "Do we really need to worry about the future when we could just focus on the present? You wanted to watch that damn movie we just did... did you not learn anything from it at all?"

"What are you trying to say? How can I not worry about the future?" I'm appalled that he would really suggest that the future wouldn't matter when it comes to something as serious as messing around together. "You know I have to plan everything out. I have a literal plan for my life. There's no way that that'd be good for me."

"Olivia. You just made me watch a movie where their time was shortened. They could have died just from being near each other, yet they still lived on the edge and risked it all. Aren't there somethings that are worth taking a risk for?"

"Yeah, but—"

Sterling abruptly cuts me off. "Nothing is guaranteed, Olivia. I know I asked you to think about it after the other night but it doesn't seem like you've really thought about it at all. If you don't want anything to do with me, I get it. I'm not asking for much. Just your time in the present."

I stare back at him, a mixture of feelings coursing through me. Of course I want to just agree with it and go along for the ride. He thinks I haven't put any thought into it, but he's wrong. I haven't been able to think about anything else, really. He's had my sole focus and I've been running every possible scenario through my mind.

"And then what happens when the present turns

into the future? You graduate and I'm just left behind?"

"Absolutely not." He shakes his head, frowning at me. "What I'm really saying is that I want to spend time with you, one-on-one time that doesn't belong to anyone else. And we will just figure it all out as we go along."

"So, we're not involved with anyone else during this time but we don't have a real label?" I question him, trying to get a real picture on what he's saying. "Basically a no-strings-attached type of deal, as far as the future goes."

Sterling flashes his perfectly straight white teeth in a grin that he doesn't often show. "See, you get exactly what I'm saying."

I look back at Sterling, not sure that I fully agree with what he's saying, but I do understand it. I don't want to be his little secret, but that's not what it sounds like he's getting at. He just doesn't want to have any commitments, anything in the future that could potentially hold him down or tie him up.

I get it, I do. Especially with the way he is about hockey and how he wants to play professionally. But is it fair to my heart to subject it to the inevitable pain it's going to endure when this is over?

"I can do that for now, Sterling," I tell him, the

honesty heavy in my voice. "But I can't make any promises for how I handle the future."

"Just don't get too attached." He winks at me, playing it off as if we're not talking about anything serious here. It's like he didn't just tell me to fall in love with him instead...

This is going to be a mindfuck I may never survive.

CHAPTER SIXTEEN
STERLING

I'm not entirely sure Olivia is completely on board with what I've proposed and I can't say that I blame her. She may wear a mask and attempt to be a complete people pleaser, but it's almost as if her guard comes down when she's around me. Only around me is she able to be completely honest with both of us.

She's pretending right now, though, and I can see right through the facade. She's putting on a brave face, trying to appease me because she doesn't want to disagree with me. It's almost like she's holding a palm full of sand, attempting to keep it from slipping through the cracks between her fingers.

And I'm as much of a liar as her right now.

We're already both too invested, but neither of us are going to be the ones to admit it first.

Taking my chance, I move closer to her. I watch the column of her throat move as she swallows nervously. Her eyes are trained on mine, bouncing back and forth. Reaching out for her, I gently cup the side of her face, my thumb stroking her smooth, soft skin.

"You don't have to be afraid of me, baby," I murmur, watching her eyelids flutter closed. She turns her body to face me, her eyelids lifting as her gaze collides with mine.

"I'm not afraid of you. I'm afraid of what you'll do to me and what it will mean for my heart."

My throat constricts, my heart pounding rapidly in my chest. "I can't promise what the future will hold, but I will never intentionally hurt you."

"I know," she whispers. She's silent for a moment, as if she's trying to decide what to do, before she goes and shocks both of us. She lifts up onto her knees, moving on top of me as she positions herself on my lap. Both of her hands are on my shoulders and she's staring down at me with those hazel eyes wide open. "Do your worst to me, Sterling."

My hand falls away from the side of her face and

I'm gripping her hips as she wraps her arms around the back of my neck. Her face dips down to mine, our mouths crashing together at once. She's in control right now and I love it. I like seeing Olivia like this. The timid, quiet girl that I've known my entire life is finally taking what she wants.

And she isn't fucking holding back.

She nips at my bottom lip before I part them to let her in. She slides her tongue across the wounds that she inflicted in my flesh before sliding it against mine. Our mouths melt together and she moves in my lap, her pussy grinding against my erection through the layers of clothing that are separating us.

Our tongues tangle together and we're lost in the moment as I steal the air from her lungs. Olivia is in the process of completely consuming me and she has no fucking clue what she's doing to me. She's driving me crazy with the way she moves in my lap. My grip tightens on her, my fingers digging into her flesh as I hold on to her hips.

She stills in my lap, her mouth breaking apart from mine as she stares down with a worried look washing over her irises. "Was I doing something wrong?"

My eyes drop down to her chest, watching it rise and fall with every shallow breath that escapes her. I can't help the grin that plays on my lips, knowing I'm the one who has this effect on her, who has left her completely breathless.

"Not at all, baby," I assure her, my hands sliding down to cup her ass as I lift her slightly. In one fluid movement, I flip her onto her back so that I'm positioned between her legs, hovering above her. "You're doing quite the opposite and it's driving me wild."

A pink tint creeps across her cheeks and she gives me a shy smile. "I'm nowhere near as experienced as you are."

"I know you had a boyfriend in high school," I say, my voice low. "You can't tell me you didn't do anything with him."

Olivia shakes her head, her eyes searching mine. "How did you know I had a boyfriend?" she questions me, her eyebrows tugging together. She doesn't wait for my response before she continues. "We messed around but we didn't have sex. Anytime that it got close to anything more than making out and feeling each other up, I had to shut him down. I couldn't let it progress any further."

Her response catches me off guard. I don't bother responding to how I know she had a boyfriend. She probably didn't really push it because she already knows the answer to her question. Of course my sister told me about it. Stella has this fun way of rambling when no one really cares. But anytime she ever brought up Olivia, she always had my attention.

"Why didn't it ever go any further, Olivia?" I ask her, my voice soft as I trail my fingers across her throat and along her jawline.

Her throat bobs as she swallows roughly. Her eyes are still attached to mine and it feels almost as if she's looking directly into my soul. I want to know why, I want her to let me in and tell me her deepest, darkest secrets. I want to know everything that goes on in that pretty little head of hers, but most importantly I want answers for why she always stopped her boyfriend when things were progressing.

"Tell me all your secrets, baby," I murmur, cupping the side of her face as my face dips down to hers. I nip at her bottom lip and she moves underneath me, a gasp slips from her. "Bury them deep inside of me and I'll take them to the fucking grave."

"He wasn't you," she whispers, her breath skating across my skin. "It didn't feel right and I didn't want him to have any of my firsts."

Lifting my head, I stare down at the beautiful girl beneath me. The one I've known almost all my life. The one who has been closer than anyone else has ever gotten. She's burying her secrets inside my soul as she burrows herself into my heart and makes a home.

I figured at one point that Olivia had a crush on me but hearing her speak the words aloud has me in my feels. My heart crawls into my throat and I can't swallow it back down. A rush of adrenaline courses through my veins and I'm lost in her eyes for a moment.

"Who were you saving your firsts for, Olivia?"

Her eyes bounce back and forth between mine before her gaze focuses on me. "You."

Abandoning her face, I bring my hand down to the bottom hem of her shirt and begin to push it up her torso. My fingers slide across her skin, feeling every inch of her. Her body trembles beneath my touch and a ghost of a smile tugs on the corners of my lips.

"Has anyone ever touched you like this?"

Olivia bites her bottom lip and nods her head. "Yeah, but that's not what I was talking about."

"Show me what you mean, sunshine."

She nods, a fire burning in her eyes. I want to dive into the flames and burn alive. She slowly pushes me away as she sits up. My hands are still on her torso, feeling her skin beneath my palms. Olivia grabs my wrists, using my hands to push her shirt up. She abandons her grip on me and I continue where she was guiding me, lifting her shirt up over her head.

I toss it onto the floor, watching her with my jaw clenched as she reaches around her back to undo her bra. My tongue darts out to wet my lips as she removes it and throws the bra onto the floor. Her eyes are on mine, wide with a mixture of excitement and nervousness.

Following her lead, I remove my own shirt and throw it onto the floor. It isn't the same as her being naked from the waist up, but at least she isn't the only one now. Olivia reaches for my wrists again, guiding my hands to her breasts, and I cup both of them in my palms. Her skin feels like silk as I stroke my thumbs over her pebbled nipples.

A moan slips from her lips and an inferno continues to blaze in her eyes. Dropping my mouth to one of her breasts, I pull her nipple into my mouth, swirling my tongue around it as I continue to knead her flesh with my hand. Olivia arches her back, pressing her chest closer to my face. Her hand is in my hair as I suck and taste her skin before moving to the other breast.

Lifting my head from her chest, our gazes collide

and I press my lips to hers, capturing her mouth with mine. Our tongues are tangled together, her hands in my hair as she holds on to me for dear life, as if she's afraid I'll slip away.

Breaking apart, I pull away from her and lift myself off the bed. "Lay back for me, baby," I murmur, reaching for her hips as she obeys. She lies back on the mattress and I strip her of her pants and underwear. My eyes trail over her body, my cock straining against my sweatpants as I drink in every goddamn inch of her.

"You're fucking beautiful, Olivia."

She swallows hard, her eyes meeting mine. "Don't stop touching me, Sterling."

The corners of my lips lift. "Never, baby."

Leaning forward, I hook my arms under her legs and drag her to the edge of the bed. A gasp escapes her and a chuckle rumbles in my chest as I drop down onto my knees. Her pussy is in my face and it takes everything in me to not devour her instantly.

Dipping my face to the apex of her thighs, I press my lips to hers before lifting my head to look up at her. "Has anyone ever touched you like this, baby? Have they ever tasted how fucking sweet you are?"

She shakes her head, a ragged breath slipping

from her lips as her chest rises and falls rapidly. "I never wanted anyone to except you."

"And no one else ever will," I murmur as I bury my face between her legs. She tastes like candy as I slide my tongue along her. Her hips buck and she lets out a soft moan as I swipe my tongue over her clit. I want to devour her, to push her past the point of ecstasy. I want her so lost in pleasure that no one can ever find her but me.

Moving my mouth against her, I devour her pussy. Licking, sucking, tasting the most sensitive part of her body. I roll my tongue across her clit, flicking it over and over. Olivia's hands find my hair and her hips involuntarily buck again.

"Oh my god, Sterling," she moans as I continue to move my tongue against her. A smirk plays on my lips and my cock throbs with need. I need to be inside her, but I need her to come all over my tongue first.

Dragging my tongue from the bottom to the top of her, I pause when I reach her clit. Drawing it in between my lips, I roll my tongue around it while simultaneously sucking on her flesh. She's a mess of moans, writhing under my touch as I continue to fuck her with my mouth. Taking a finger, I slide it along her center, slowly pressing it inside as I play with her clit.

Olivia's slowly coming undone, her orgasm building deep inside as I begin to pump my finger in and out of her pretty pussy. She's so fucking tight, so fucking wet. Jesus Christ, I'm going to get so lost in her, and I'm completely fine with that.

"That's it, baby," I murmur against her pussy as I curl my finger inside of her, pressing against the soft pad of flesh inside. "Come for me. I want to taste you on my tongue."

"I'm so close, Sterling." She lets out a strangled moan, her hands gripping my hair tighter. "Don't stop."

"Let go for me, Olivia. Let me be the one who brings you the most pleasure."

I dive back in, my mouth suctioned to her pussy as I move my tongue around her clit. My finger moves in and out of her, stroking her G-spot every time. It isn't long before her pussy is clenching my finger and she's crying out. Her orgasm hits her fucking hard, her entire body shattering as I taste her on my tongue.

Her body shakes as an earthquake of pleasure tears through her. Her legs are quaking, her thighs clamping the sides of my head as I continue to lick and suck her arousal. Slowly drawing my finger from her pussy, I release her from my mouth. My chin is wet from her release and I wipe it away with the back of my hand as I rise to my feet.

Olivia lays on the bed, her legs spread wide open as she stares up at me with a dazed look in her eyes. "That was the most amazing thing I've ever felt."

Reaching for the waistband of my pants, I begin to push them and my boxer briefs down my thighs. "That's just the beginning, sunshine."

She lifts her heavy head, her eyes dropping down to my cock as I inch closer to her. "Wait, Sterling."

I pause at the edge of the bed, my heart in my throat as I tilt my head to the side. "What's wrong, baby? We don't have to if you aren't ready."

"No, it's not that," she shakes her head, a pink tint creeping across her cheeks. "I don't think it's going to fit. I mean, I don't know. You're big... like, really big."

A chuckle rumbles in my chest. "I promise you we can make it fit. And I'll try my best not to hurt you."

Her throat bobs as she swallows hard before lifting her gaze back to mine. "I trust you, Sterling," she says softly, a smile pulling on her lips. "And I want you more than anything."

Crawling up onto the bed, I settle between her legs. Planting my hands on either side of her head, I stare down at her as the tip of my cock presses against her soaked pussy. "Are you on birth control? Because I want to feel you without anything between us."

Olivia nods. "I am."

"Thank God," I breathe out a sigh of relief. "Are you good with that, sunshine?"

She nods again. "I don't want anything between us either. I want to feel you inside me... every inch."

An involuntary groan escapes me and I feel like I could explode in this instance. Keeping my eyes on hers, I slowly push inside her. She gasps, her eyes widening as I stop halfway before pulling out slightly. "I'm going to work myself in to help with the pain. It might be uncomfortable, but I promise I'll take care of you, my sweet girl."

She looks up at me with nothing but trust in her eyes. My heart swells as it pounds erratically in my chest. I've never been anyone's first before and I can't believe that I'm hers. Words can't describe the emotions that are building within me right now.

There's literally nothing that comes close to touching how this moment feels with her.

Slowly easing into her, she lets out another gasp as I begin with shallow, slow thrusts. With each one, I inch in deeper. Her legs wrap around my waist and I drop down onto my forearms as I capture her lips with my own. Maybe if I can distract her with my mouth, it will help ease her pain and let her focus solely on the pleasure.

Her tongue slides against mine and I steal the air from her lungs as I continue to slowly fuck her tight pussy. She clenches around me and I press into her deeper, swallowing her moans. Her body stills and I know in that moment that I officially took her virginity. And she willingly handed this moment over to me.

Drawing my hips back, I pull out a little bit before sliding back into her. Her legs tighten around my waist and her hands are on my back. Her nails dig into my skin as she suddenly becomes overwhelmed with pleasure since she's able to ignore any discomfort.

I'm so close to exploding, I don't know how much longer I can hold it in with the way her pussy tightens around me. She's so wet and I feel the warmth beginning to flood my body. My balls are constricting, drawing closer to my body as I pick up the speed, fucking her with an urgency.

She's moaning in my mouth as her tongue tangles with mine, and it isn't long before she's writhing underneath me. Her pussy feels like a vise grip, tightening around my cock as she shatters into a million pieces around me. That's all it takes to send me over the edge. I had every intention of pulling out, but I can't stop myself as my orgasm hits me like a fucking Mack truck.

I lose myself in her completely and we both free fall into the abyss of euphoria.

I'm drowning in her and I never want to come up for air.

CHAPTER SEVENTEEN
OLIVIA

I didn't go to Sterling's house with the intention of sleeping there. But after the two orgasms he gave me back to back, I was completely spent. He was my first and I wouldn't have wanted it to happen any other way. I would do it over again and again if I could.

I want him to be my first when it comes to everything.

When I wake up in the morning, the sunlight is shining brightly through his window. Rolling over in bed, I see that Sterling is already awake. He's lying beside me, a lazy grin on his lips as he watches me from where he's laying.

"You know, you snore a lot," he muses out loud with a look of amusement in his eyes.

My eyebrows tug together and I roll my eyes at him. "No, I don't."

Sterling chuckles as he slides his arm underneath my neck and pulls me closer to him. He rolls onto his back, pulling me flush against his side. Our naked bodies are once again pressed together. I can't help but want to explore more of him, but after last night I'm fairly sore. Sterling was a perfect gentleman and tended to me afterward, making sure that I was comfortable and not in any pain.

I like this sweet side of him—the one that is reserved for only me.

"What do you have to do today?" he questions me, his voice soft as he traces invisible patterns on my naked back with the tips of his fingers.

"Nothing," I answer him as I wrap my arm around his torso. My face is pressed against his chest and I feel like I could spend an eternity in his arms. Even though the future is completely unpredictable, I like these moments with him. I'm content with this, even if this is all I will ever get from him. "Do you have anything going on?"

"I actually have a game later tonight, but I was wondering if maybe you would want to come back over afterward." There's a nervousness in his voice that I've never heard before and it makes me smile. I like the vulnerable side of Sterling. It shows that there's more to him than what meets the eye and I love every single one of his layers, regardless of how rough they might be around the edges.

"I would love that," I tell him, turning my head to face him as I rest my chin on his chest. "I should probably get home and get a shower and everything. I'm sure you have a lot to do to get ready for your game."

Sterling's lips part slightly like he's about to say something, and there's a part of me that wishes he would invite me to his game. Then again, why would he? It's not like we have anything definitive between us, and that means he would be inviting me into his world even more. He might not be ready for that and if he isn't, then I'm not going to push anything either.

I only want to be a part of his world when he's ready to let me in completely.

If that ever happens...

"I'll take you back to your dorm whenever you're ready," he says gently as if he's tiptoeing around me. I swallow back the disappointment and nod as I move away from him.

"I'll get dressed and then I'm ready to go when you are."

Sterling flashes me that smile he keeps hidden from the rest of the world as he climbs out of bed. We both get dressed in silence and he hands me my coat as he takes my backpack and leaves the bedroom. I follow after him, walking down the hallway. Thankfully, I don't have to do the walk of shame in front of his roommates because neither of them are anywhere to be seen.

I follow Sterling out into the cold air, which is a stark contrast to the bright sun shining from above. Pausing by his car, I close my eyes and tilt my head back to soak up the warmth. The sun is one of my favorite things about life. Mainly because it brings everything around us to life. You can't help but smile when you feel the warmth of its rays soaking into your soul.

As I open my eyes and move my head, I catch Sterling watching me from his side of the car. There's an unreadable expression on his face and emotion swirls in his irises. He doesn't say anything as he gets in behind the wheel and I follow suit, climbing into the passenger's side.

We're both quiet and lost in our thoughts as we head back to campus. It feels like the car ride is shorter than I've ever experienced. Suddenly, he's pulling up in front of the building and it's time for us to go our separate ways. There's an awkwardness that settles heavily in the air around us and I shift nervously in my seat before turning toward the door.

"Thanks for last night and the ride home," I tell Sterling, glancing at him over my shoulder as I reach for the door handle. Just as I'm about to pull it, I feel his hands on my shoulders, pulling me back to face him.

Sterling releases my shoulders as I'm now facing him and he cups the sides of my face. "Don't go like that, sunshine," he murmurs, stroking my cheeks. "Never leave me like that."

"Like what?"

"Without a kiss," he says softly, his face dipping down to mine. He kisses me with a tenderness, his tongue gently caressing mine as he effectively steals the air from my lungs. Releasing me, we break apart as we both come up for air. I'm left breathless, with his mark left on my soul.

"I'll call you after my game, okay?" he says, his eyes bouncing back and forth between mine like he's searching for my approval.

"That sounds perfect." I smile at him as I open the door. "Good luck tonight," I say as I get out of the car.

"Get some rest because I plan on showing you some new things tonight," he says with a wink as I shut the door. Clenching my thighs together, I attempt to feign off the friction that builds. I've never felt this way about anyone else and it honestly scares the hell out of me.

What happens when this all goes up in flames?

I'll be left to pick up the ashes myself...

———

After taking a hot shower and a nap, I'm lying on my bed reading when my phone goes off. Glancing at the alarm clock on my nightstand, I notice it's only four o'clock in the afternoon, so it isn't Sterling. His game probably hasn't even started yet.

Grabbing my phone, I pick it up and look at the name on the screen.

Noah.

My stomach sinks as memories of last night bombard my mind. The last conversation I had with Noah, he asked about Sterling and I told him that Sterling was just a friend. And then I went and ended up in bed with him last night. I need to tell Noah the truth and let him go. He's the safer option but it isn't fair to him. I can't lead him on, stringing him along as a second option when everything with Sterling goes south.

"Hello?" I answer the phone with my stomach in knots. I don't know how the hell I'm going to tell him.

"Hey! How are you, Olivia?"

I practically choke on the air that I attempt to exhale. "I'm um, good. How are you?"

"I'm good. I was just wondering if you wanted to do something this evening. I feel like it's been a while since we've hung out and I wanted to see you."

My stomach sinks as dread rolls in the pit of my stomach. I want to hang out with him as friends, but nothing more. I feel terrible thinking about what I need to tell him and saying it to him now on the phone. I should just meet with him and have a real conversation face to face, instead of through the phone.

"I have plans later tonight, but I'm not doing anything this evening if you wanted to get together."

"That sounds perfect." I can hear the smile in his voice and it only makes me feel worse. "I'll pick you up at six and we can go do something."

I can't help but feel terrible already and have

instant regret. "That sounds good to me. I'll see you then."

After ending the call, I set my phone back on my nightstand before rolling over onto my stomach. I bury my face in my pillow and fight the urge to scream. Sterling won't be happy if he knows I'm hanging out with Noah before seeing him, but he should be happy when he finds out I've told Noah that there can't ever be anything between us.

I spend the next hour in bed staring at my ceiling before it's time for me to get ready. I put on a light layer of makeup and dress in something warm with the way the temperature drops here at night. I don't know what Noah has planned, but I want to make sure I'm warm enough.

And I need to figure out when exactly I'm going to break the news to him tonight.

Noah, being himself, is promptly waiting outside at six o'clock on the dot. With my scarf wrapped tightly around my neck, I shove my gloved hands into the pockets of my coat as I walk through the brisk air toward his car. He gets out and opens the door for me as I reach the vehicle.

I climb inside, regret building within me as I put on my seat belt. Noah slides in behind the wheel, turning to face me with that damn bright smile on his face.

"I'm glad you wore something warm," he tells me as he puts on his own seat belt and puts the car in drive.

My eyebrows pull together and I tilt my head to the side. "Why's that?"

Noah's smile is warm. "We're going to go watch a hockey game tonight."

My stomach falls to the floor as dread consumes me. No, this can't happen. We can't go to the hockey game. We can't go there because Sterling will be there and if he sees us together, this isn't going to go well at all.

"I don't really care for sports," I tell him, shrugging as I attempt to be dismissive.

Noah's face falls. "My brother plays on the opposing team and I told him I would come tonight. If you don't want to come to the game with me, that's okay. I would never make you do something you don't want to do."

Damn Noah and his moral code.

Plastering a smile to my face, I shake my head. "No, it's okay. I'll go with you."

I instantly regret the words as they fall from my lips, but it's too late now. I already agreed to go with him because I don't want to disappoint him. I'm already going to be telling him that we can't be anything more than friends. The least I can do is go to a game with him...

And pray to God that Sterling doesn't see us.

CHAPTER EIGHTEEN
STERLING

Olivia Davis is in my head, she's under my skin; she's in my goddamn soul right now. I'm nowhere close to having my fill of her. She's been in my bed, I've tasted every inch of her skin. I don't know that I'll ever be able to get her out of my system now. I thought I could fuck her out of it, but I was wrong... so terribly wrong.

I haven't seen her since this morning and it's been driving me absolutely insane. We've been talking and I've been trying really hard to not come on too strong. The last thing I want to do is scare her away. Olivia is constantly looking for an exit route just in case of an emergency, regardless of what it could possibly be.

And I can tell by the way that Olivia responds,

she's about to go into fight-or-flight mode at any given moment. Olivia doesn't fight, she just fucking runs in the opposite direction of anything that could potentially be a threat.

Which includes me.

"Yo, you almost ready?" Logan calls over to me as I finish putting my gear on for tonight's game. We're getting closer to the championship games for the season, so we've really been working on our team structure and the way we play together.

"Yeah, I just gotta grab my stick and gloves," I tell him as I rise up onto my skates. Logan is the last one left in the locker room as the rest of the guys already headed out to warm up before the game starts.

"Well, hurry the hell up," he scolds me, acting like my goddamn parent. "You know Coach is going to be pissed if we're all stuck waiting on your ass."

I watch him disappear through the doorway as I slide my hands into my gloves and grab my stick. Walking on my skates, I head out into the tunnel and make my way to the rink. The arena is already full of spectators—most being friends and family or students from Wyncote. Our hockey team is pretty popular with the school since we're the main sport the university is known for.

As I step out onto the ice, everyone is already warming up, shooting pucks at our goalie, Asher. Skating over to the other guys, I stretch my legs for a moment before grabbing my own puck with the blade of my stick. Pushing it back and forth with the front and back of my stick, I keep my eyes on the net and begin to skate toward Asher.

I continue to stickhandle it, attempting to fake him out as he drops down into the butterfly stance. Flicking my wrist, I shoot my shot and send the puck soaring into the top shelf of the net. Asher swears at me, rising back onto his feet as the other guys begin to send shots in his direction.

We practice for another few moments before it's time to head over to the bench for the game to start. I take a seat next to August and Logan, who are both staring out onto the ice, waiting to head back out. They're two of our best players, so they are usually the first ones out on the ice. I tend to come in during the second shift.

Since the shifts only last about forty-five seconds, it's not like I have to wait long to get my chance out there, but any ice time is precious. You don't take that shit for granted, regardless of how long or short it actually is.

Coach tells both of them to head out as the

other team sends their players out. Asher is already at the goal as Logan makes his way to the defensive zone. I watch as August bends his knees, getting closer to the ice with his stick, ready to go as he lines up for the face-off with the opposing center player.

The ref drops the puck and they begin to fight over it, each of them battling against one another to win the face-off. August manages to get the puck away from the other player and sends it back to our zone, where Hayden catches it with the toe of his stick. He begins to skate toward the center of the ice, everyone following along with him as they make their way into the other team's zone.

It doesn't take long before it's my turn to head out into the game. We didn't score a goal so the puck ends up getting passed back and forth between our team and the other. As I step out onto the ice, I begin to skate until my legs are burning, heading over to where the play already is. I hang back, staying away from the middle pack as I slap the ice with my stick, calling for the puck.

Vaughn has it and his eyes find me through the group that's around him. He manages to break free, passing the puck over to me when he gets the chance. The other team's side is essentially open as they were all battling over the puck instead of playing the ice smart.

Pushing off with my skates, I move as fast as I can, stickhandling the puck as I slide effortlessly into the other team's defensive zone. None of their defensemen are around and it's just the goalie and me in this moment. This is my chance and I can't risk fucking it up.

I will never compare to August or Vaughn and the way they play offense, but it's my turn to get some recognition too.

The goalie gets into his stance and it only takes one deke to get him to go butterfly. He's known for having a weak glove and I send the puck into the top shelf of the net. The horn blares through the speakers and all of the guys on my team instantly rush me as everyone is fucking pumped. I typically get some assists and score some goals during our games, but having the first goal that puts us on the board is a phenomenal feeling.

It's time for our shift change, so I begin to skate over toward the bench again as August and Logan are climbing over the board. Lifting my eyes, my gaze finds the stands and I mindlessly look around, not looking for anyone in particular.

And then I see her.

And my entire world fucking freezes.

My throat constricts and it feels like a punch directly in my gut when I see Olivia sitting next to the same asshole I told her to get rid of. I didn't invite her to my game, so I don't know why the hell she's here. Not to mention the fact that she's here with another guy.

My mind is blown in this moment and I don't realize that I'm standing in place until the guys begin to yell at me to get off the ice. The last thing we need is a penalty for too many guys on the ice, but I can't seem to fucking move.

She's not mine—we're not together.

I try to keep reminding myself that, chanting it over and over in my mind like a mantra. It might be true, but I expressed my distaste for him. I've barely even touched her, but I can't help but feel a sense of possessiveness when it comes to Olivia. She's always been the one who's been under my skin.

And this... this feels like a punch to the fucking throat.

"I swear to God, Sterling," Simon growls at me from the bench as he leans over it. "Move your fucking feet before one of us carries you off the ice."

My eyes meet his and I'm brought back to reality. My legs begin to move involuntarily as I skate over to the bench and hop over the boards before taking my seat next to my teammates. They're all bitching at me, but I don't even hear the words they're saying.

The fucked up thing about reality is that Olivia is with that asshole.

And I don't like it one bit.

CHAPTER NINETEEN
OLIVIA

My stomach sinks, falling to the floor once again when my gaze collides with Sterling's. The bile rises up my throat as I'm overcome with dread. I can't help but feel like I'm ready to take off out of this damn arena right now. I knew this was a mistake and I shouldn't have come here with Noah.

Judging by the way Sterling was looking at the two of us, he was not happy at all. I already know he got the wrong impression and I can only imagine what is going through his mind right now. There's no doubt in my mind that he's currently thinking I betrayed him.

And can we talk about how messed up it is that I would come to his game with another guy?

I know exactly how it looks, and it doesn't look good. It's definitely only going to create problems between the two of us and we're just getting started. I wish I could punch myself right now for being so stupid. And I haven't even gotten the chance to talk to Noah about what I wanted to talk with him about.

"Are you okay?" Noah questions me, his head tilting to the side with a concerned look in his eyes. "You don't look like you're feeling so well."

"I don't, actually," I tell him, and it isn't completely a lie. I need to get the hell out of here and it's almost making me feel physically ill. "If you don't mind, I think I'm going to head home."

I glance out at the ice and I see Sterling skating back on. Instead of going to take his position, he's power skating towards one of the players on the other team and it isn't long before they're throwing their gloves onto the ice.

"Olivia," Noah says my name again, pulling my attention away from the shit show that is unfolding on the ice. "I can give you a ride back to your dorm."

I have to get out of here. I glance back at the game and see Sterling getting pulled away from the other player. I look back at Noah.

Shaking my head at him, I raise my hand dismissively. "No, you stay. That way you can see your brother afterward. I'll get an Uber, I don't mind at all."

"Are you absolutely sure?" he questions me, not letting the issue go. "I feel really terrible not giving you a ride back."

"I'm positive, Noah," I tell him, offering a small smile. "You stay and enjoy yourself and I'll talk to you another time."

I'm going to have to wait to tell him the truth, because right now all I can think about is the way Sterling was looking at the two of us. And my intense need to flee from this place right now. This is what happens when things aren't the way I want them to be. This is why I play life safe. When it comes down to feeling uncomfortable, my flight instincts kick in and I bolt.

Just like I'm doing right now. I'm running away from Noah and from Sterling.

I don't know what will come of this and that's what scares me the most.

———

After waiting outside for about fifteen minutes, I'm finally sitting in the back seat of an Uber on my way back to campus. I should just text Noah and tell him the truth. I really messed up by not at least having that conversation with him. It's going to make things worse with Sterling when he approaches me about being at the game.

And I know damn well he's going to because this isn't something he would easily let go.

He's going to want answers. And I'm not going to have the ones he's wanting to hear. I'm afraid of what he's going to say, how he's going to react to this. I don't see anything good coming from this. But I'm left with no choice but to wait to hear from Sterling.

And that's if he even bothers calling me after his game now...

By the time I get home, my stomach is in knots and I don't know what to do with myself. I end up in my dorm room, where thankfully my roommate isn't here again. I begin to pace, walking around the small space like a caged animal. I don't even feel like I can be here right now.

And if I'm being honest, I don't feel like there's anywhere I can go and feel comfortable right now. My childhood home and my family aren't that far away, but the last thing I want to do is go back there because I have a problem that I don't know how to deal with.

Putting my coat back on again, I head back out of my dorm and into the frigid air of the night. It's cold outside—too cold to be walking around—but I refuse to sit around in my dorm right now when I'm essentially waiting for a bomb to detonate.

I don't know how long I've been walking around campus before I head out onto the street. There isn't much traffic and there isn't any foot traffic right now. I'm all alone as I walk down the sidewalk, hugging myself with my coat wrapped tightly around my body to feign off the cold.

I'm not sure I even feel it as it rattles my bones, sending shivers up my spine. My teeth chatter and I feel the burn against my cheeks, but all I can really feel right now is the anxiety that is building deep inside me.

My phone begins to vibrate in my pocket and I pull it out, my stomach sinking as I see his name on the screen. I wasn't sure if Sterling would call me or not, but lo and behold, there he is. I'm not sure if I'm ready to face him right now, even though I didn't do anything wrong.

Ignoring the call, I keep my phone in my hand as

I continue to walk. It rings again and I still don't answer. I'm not afraid of him, but I'm afraid of facing reality. He asked a simple thing of me and I couldn't even do that. If anything, I'm almost more ashamed of myself.

My phone vibrates again, but this time with a text message. Stopping in the middle of the sidewalk, I inhale deeply as I unlock my screen and tap on the new message.

STERLING

Answer your phone, sunshine.

I let out a ragged breath and stare down at the screen as another message comes through.

STERLING

You can't outrun your problems, Olivia. We need to talk and I'm not going to leave you alone until we do.

Taking a deep breath, I close my eyes and count to ten. He's right and I know Sterling. When he has something in his mind, he's relentless and determined. There isn't anything that will deter him. He has respect, but when it comes to something serious, he won't let it go. And he's not going to let me go that easily.

Tapping on his name, I let the phone begin to ring as I hold it up to my ear. It only rings twice before I hear Sterling's voice come through.

"Olivia," he breathes, sounding half breathless with a touch of worry laced in his voice. "Where are you? I came to your dorm and you're not here."

"What are you doing there?"

"We had plans," he says as if nothing happened tonight. "Just because you were at my game with another guy doesn't mean I'm going to cancel those plans with you. You didn't answer my calls so I went in to look for you. Unless you're in there right now and you were ignoring my knocking."

"I'm not there," I admit, looking around to see where the hell I even walked to. "I'm on the corner of Washington Avenue and Decatur Street."

"What the hell are you doing there? Are you by yourself?"

A sigh slips from my lips. "Yeah. I left the game early and decided to go for a walk after I got back to my dorm."

"It's fucking freezing outside right now," he mutters, and I hear the purr of his engine through the phone as he turns on his car. "Stay where you are and I'll be right there."

"You don't have to come get me," I tell him,

defeat hanging heavily in my voice as I sit down on a bench that is along the street. "It's okay. I understand if you don't want anything to do with me after tonight."

"What the hell are you talking about?" he demands, the frustration laced in his question. "Olivia. There's nothing you could do that would make me not want anything to do with you."

"But I was there with Noah after you asked me to stop hanging out with him."

Sterling sighs. "We will talk in a minute. I'm almost there."

"Okay," I half whisper into the phone. I'm not so sure I want to see him right now, but he's right. We do need to talk about this. Noah is one of my closest friends and if I can maintain that relationship with him, I would like to do that. But at the same time, I want to respect Sterling. I don't want him to be questioning things and not trusting me.

He stays on the phone with me, even though we're both silent, until he's pulling his car up along the side of the street. I'm still sitting on the bench and I can feel the cold penetrating my bones at this point. Sterling hops out of his car as I rise to my feet and he meets me halfway on the sidewalk. He quickly takes off his coat and wraps it around my shoulders before ushering me over to the vehicle.

He walks me to the passenger's side, opening the door for me before helping me into the car. I don't need his help, but I accept it anyway. I just want to feel his closeness right now. To know that everything is going to be okay and this isn't going to cause a divide between the two of us.

Sterling closes the door and rushes over to his side before climbing in behind the steering wheel. He cranks on the heat and turns on the heater for my seat before pulling away from the curb.

"I'm taking you back to my place, baby," he murmurs, reaching over for my frozen hand. He laces our fingers together and slowly strokes my thumb with his own. His knuckles are bruised and battered from his fight earlier. "We need to get you warm."

"I'm fine, Sterling," I tell him, my teeth still chattering as I attempt to thaw out from the frigid air. "I'm sorry I was there with Noah. I didn't know he wanted to go to the game until we were already leaving campus."

Sterling's jaw tics. His lip is busted open and there's a bruise forming under his eye. "What were you doing with him? I thought you were done with him."

"I am…" My voice trails off for a moment. "I was going to tell him tonight that I just want to be friends with him, but I didn't get the chance to."

"Why not?"

"Because I left the game after seeing you. I took an Uber home."

Sterling snorts. "The asshole couldn't even give you a ride home?"

"I told him to stay. His brother was playing on the other team and I didn't want him to miss it on my account. I plan on telling him next time I see him."

A harsh laugh escapes Sterling and I turn my head to look at him, my eyebrows drawn together. "Of course his brother plays on the losing team," he laughs again, shaking his head. "You don't have to worry about telling him. I saw him after the game and made sure he knows his place now."

I stare at him, my eyes wide. "You did what? You had no right doing that. Do you not know what boundaries are?"

Sterling doesn't look back at me. "I told you if you didn't get rid of him that I would."

This harshness is the side of Sterling that I don't

like. He's been more positive since we've been spending time together and this is the side of him I prefer to avoid like the plague. He's not necessarily being mean to me, but he isn't nice at all when he's like this.

"Please take me home, Sterling."

He turns his attention back to the road. "That's what I'm doing, baby."

"No, not to your home. To mine. Take me back to my dorm room. I don't want to be around you when you're being like this."

"Being like what?" he questions me, turning his head back to look at me as he stops at a red light. "I'm sorry for being a little pissed off at seeing you with that asshole. I thought we had an agreement and that you weren't going to be spending time with him."

"You're being mean and I don't like this side of you. You keep calling him an asshole, but it's really you who is the asshole," I tell him, watching his eyes widen. It isn't often that I swear and for me to be directing my anger at him is something new too. Gone is the sunshine Olivia. Now, Sterling's going to meet the bitchier side of me who is fed up with his little temper tantrum. "Noah is actually a really nice guy, but he's not the one I want. Stop being an idiot and realize that you are the one I want. You have no reason to be intimidated by him."

"I'm not intimidated by him. I just don't appreciate another guy pining after the girl I want to be with."

"You don't even want me to be with you, Sterling!" I raise my voice and I catch myself off guard, but it's too late to stop it now. "You just want me to boost your ego or feed your sick sense of doing something different. I'm the good girl you want to turn naughty. I'm not going to put up with you acting like I'm your territory."

"Olivia, listen," he quickly starts to backtrack as he begins to drive down the road again. "I'm sorry for overreacting. I just don't like it because I know he has feelings for you. I would feel better about it if the two of you were just friends."

"So, why can't you just say that to me instead? Why do you have to be such a dick about it instead of being honest? Would it really kill you to let someone in and see the real side of you instead of putting on your asshole mask?" I pause, letting out an exasperated sigh. "Please, just take me back to my dorm. I don't want to be with you tonight."

Sterling's eyes are wide as he stares at me for a

moment. I watch his throat bob as he swallows nervously. "You really want me to take you back?"

"That's what I said, isn't it?" I snap at him. I instantly regret it, but screw him. He's been enough of an asshole tonight and I don't want to deal with it. I talked to him and said what I needed to. Now, I need some time to breathe that doesn't involve breathing in the same air as him.

"Okay," he sighs in defeat, "I'll take you home."

We fall into an uncomfortable silence as he turns the car around and begins to head back to campus. My heart is thick with emotions and I'm struggling to keep them back. There's a lump lodged in my throat and it feels like a damn rock that I can't get out. Tears prick at the corners of my eyes and I'm fighting them back with all of my might.

The last thing I'm going to do is let Sterling see me cry after this.

I'm filled with emotion and even more disappointed in myself right now. It isn't often that I lose my cool and freak out on someone, but I let my emotions get the better of me in this moment. I just wish we could both see from each other's point of view. Or at least meet in the middle. I think Sterling realizes he was wrong, but now we're both left feeling the regret of our behavior.

As we pull up to the dorm building, Sterling pulls his car along the curb and puts it in park before turning to face me. "I really am sorry, Olivia. I completely overreacted instead of talking to you first." He pauses for a moment. "I shouldn't have expected the worst and let it get the better of me."

"I'm sorry for the way I reacted too," I tell him, my voice quiet as I stare back at him. "I just need some space. Some time to breathe and just think."

"I understand," he practically whispers, his voice cracking around his words. "I just hope I didn't ruin things between us. I don't know. I'll give you however much space you need. I'm not going anywhere."

I nod, not fully trusting my voice. As much as I want to give in and just go back to his place, I know this is what is best. I can't let this type of behavior from either of us be rewarded. Sterling needs to learn some boundaries and I need to learn to not let him have such a hold over me.

"Goodnight, Sterling," I whisper before climbing out of the car. I catch one last look at him before shutting the door and it practically breaks my heart. He looks like someone just ripped his heart from his chest. For some reason, goodnight feels like saying goodbye.

Inhaling deeply, it takes everything in me to walk away from him. Tears are falling from my eyes as I reach the door to the building and by the time I reach my room, I'm full-on crying.

I can't help but feel like this may have been the end of us.

And we have no one to blame but ourselves.

CHAPTER TWENTY
STERLING

After a few sleepless nights, I'm practically a zombie walking through the motions of life. I've been giving Olivia her space, but I can't help but feel like she's never going to come back to me. It was a complete miscommunication and I went and fucked it up even more. I shouldn't have intervened and approached Noah about it.

Actually, the more I think about it, we were really both in the wrong, but I did much worse than her. She's right, I've been more jealous and possessive than necessary. And I know how Olivia operates. She sees that as a threat and she runs, just like she did on Saturday night.

I can't say I blame her because I was being an

unreasonable asshole, but in that moment it felt like it was a valid reason for me. I didn't like her hanging out with Noah because I have seen the way he looks at her. He looks at her like he wants to be more than friends with her, and I don't like that at all. If she doesn't want to be with him, she should have let him know.

It's not an excuse, but the tension from the game coupled with seeing the two of them together when I was under the impression she already told him they weren't hanging out like that completely threw me off. It brought out the worst of me and it's no one's fault but my own. I reacted out of emotion instead of responding rationally.

I'm not stupid. I know that Olivia wants me. Hell, she gave me the most sacred part of herself. The one thing she kept from everyone else and had reserved for me. That alone should tell me enough. I just can't help but struggle with my own insecurities. I've never felt like this about anyone else, so this is new uncharted territory for me.

It scares the shit out of me because she has the power to destroy me.

"Are you okay, Sterling?" Vaughn questions me as he walks into the living room. I'm lying on the couch, as I have been the past few days. I've been trapped in my own hell of self-loathing and there hasn't been a single thing that has made me want to come out of it.

I haven't missed any practices or any of my classes, but my interactions with anyone have been few and far between. Even with my own damn roommates.

"I'm good," I lie through my teeth like I have every other time that Simon has asked me the same question in the past few days.

"Stop bullshitting me and tell me what's up," Vaughn retorts as he sits down on the recliner and props up his feet.

"It's just this girl. It's nothing, and I'll figure it out," I tell him dismissively, not wanting to divulge all the details.

"Wait... is it the girl you had locked away in your room on Friday night?" Simon questions me as he walks into the room and drops down onto the couch. I look over at him with my eyes wide. "Don't look at me like that, dumbass. The walls in this house are thin. I heard the two of you in there and then when you took her home the next morning."

I stare at him for a moment. "Why didn't you say anything then?"

"Because it's none of my business. You don't

question me or Vaughn when we bring girls home, but then again, I don't act all fucking mopey afterward." Simon stops talking, his eyes widening. "Wait... is it that girl I saw you talking to at Wyncote the other week? Isn't that Stella's best friend?"

Closing my eyes, I let out a shallow breath as I tip my head back. "Yes."

"Holy shit. You're fucking your sister's best friend," Vaughn says, half chuckling.

Lifting my head back up, I narrow my eyes at him. "So what? Stella wouldn't give two shits."

"Would she if she knew that it was more than just fucking?" Simon questions me.

My face scrunches up. "What the hell are you talking about? We fucked around and it's done. There's nothing more to it."

"You're such a fucking liar." Simon shakes his head at me, clicking his tongue. "If it wasn't more than that, you wouldn't be acting like someone just killed your puppy right now. What happened? She kick your miserable ass to the curb."

"Something like that," I mumble.

"I'm not going to push you on the issue, dude... but you need to talk to her. You need to tell her your real feelings."

I raise an eyebrow at him. "And what do you think my real feelings are, oh wise one?"

"That you're in love with her, bro."

There's a knock on the door that breaks through our conversation. I abruptly sit up, whipping my head to the side as I look in the direction of the front door. Could it possibly be her? I haven't tried to call or text her and she hasn't done the same to me either, but maybe she decided to just show up and see me instead?

"Are either of you expecting anyone?" Vaughn questions me as he begins to walk toward the door. I'm on my feet, hot on his heels as we both stride toward the knocking sound that starts again.

"No. You're not?"

My heart swells and my hopes are instantly up. Maybe I didn't fuck things up by being an asshole. Simon and I stop behind Vaughn as he unlocks the door and pulls it open. A small form bounces through the door, practically knocking both of us over.

"Big brother!" Stella exclaims loudly, throwing her arms around my neck. I'm completely caught off guard and simultaneously feel a little deflated at the same time. "Surprise!"

Stella releases me and steps over to give Simon

and Vaughn each a hug too. Simon's arms linger around her waist for an extra second and something glimmers in his eyes as he stares down at her. She looks between the two of us with a huge smile on her face. I glance behind her, noticing a suitcase that sits just outside of the front door.

"What are you doing here?" I question her, my voice void of any emotion.

"Jesus, I thought maybe you'd be excited to see me," she mutters, rolling her eyes. Simon walks behind her, grabbing her suitcase as he brings it in and shuts the door. Vaughn makes his way back over to the couch. "I have a random week off from classes so I thought it was the perfect time to come surprise my brother and my best friend."

My heart sinks at the mention of Olivia. Of course Stella will want to see her while she's here. She wouldn't just be here to see me.

"Of course I'm excited to see you," I tell her as we all walk deeper into the house. "Just a little surprised is all. I wasn't expecting you."

Stella crosses her arms over her chest, narrowing her eyes at me slightly. "You seem grumpier than normal. What's your deal?" She turns to look between Simon and Vaughn. "What's wrong with him now?"

Simon shrugs and throws his hands up in innocence. "No idea. You gotta talk to him about that one."

Vaughn snorts but he doesn't dime me out either.

"Not right now," she says, giving me a free pass, to which I let out a sigh of relief. "We'll get into that later. But right now, I want to know everything that has been going on. And then I thought maybe you could take me over to see Olivia?"

I swallow hard over the lump in my throat, ignoring Simon's gaze that is burning into the side of my head. "That sounds like a plan."

We all file into the living room and I'm suddenly wishing that my sister would have chosen a different time to come here. Not only am I going to have to face Olivia again, but I'm probably going to end up having to tell my sister the truth...

That I'm in love with her best friend.

CHAPTER TWENTY-ONE
OLIVIA

As I walk to my class, I see that Noah isn't waiting for me. It's been like this since last weekend, when I left the hockey game and had my run-in with Sterling. Noah hasn't spoken a word to me since. He doesn't wait for me to walk into class, not even a glance in my direction. He doesn't sit anywhere near me during any of the classes we have together.

And I can't help but blame Sterling for it.

I know I should have said something to Noah sooner. I should have been proactive to protect our friendship, but I didn't. Instead, Sterling went ahead and tried to take care of it for me, but he went about it in the worst way possible. He practically acted like

I was his property and that Noah wasn't allowed to come anywhere near me.

The classroom is still fairly empty when I walk inside and I see Noah seated in his new seat that is a few rows in front of where we used to sit together. Inhaling deeply, I straighten my shoulders and walk directly toward him. As I stop in front of his desk, he doesn't lift his gaze to mine. He acts like I'm not even there.

"Hey, Noah," I say quietly, my palms sweating as I hold on to the straps of my backpack. "Can we talk?"

"Nothing to talk about," he replies gruffly, keeping his gaze down on the material in front of him. He's making me completely unsettled with the way he says it so dismissively. I don't miss the way his jaw clenches. A sigh escapes him and he finally lifts his head to look at me.

"I'm sorry about Sterling. I didn't know he would approach you or say anything to you."

Noah's eyes meet mine and he looks distant, like there's a wave of pain passing through his irises. "I don't even know what to really say about it, Olivia." He pauses for a moment, shaking his head. "I asked you if he was any kind of competition and you assured me he wasn't—that he was just a friend.

And then to have him approach me and tell me I need to back off and leave you alone was like a slap to the face."

I wince at his words, feeling the blow to my chest from the sadness that lingers in his tone. He's upset and angry, which I've never seen Noah react to something so emotionally before. I really messed up... I'm beginning to wonder if he liked me more than he let on.

"I'm sorry, Noah," I tell him, the regret laced within my words. There's literally nothing else I can say. Nothing will go back and change the way things played out. "I was meaning to tell you that I just wanted to be friends with you, and I was going to that night but didn't get the chance to."

"Because you saw him," he says, a knowing look in his eyes. "You left because you saw him on the ice."

I swallow hard over the emotion that wells in my throat. Tears prick the corners of my eyes but I refuse to let them fall. "You're right. I didn't want to go to the game because I didn't want to see him. And then he saw the two of us together and he got the wrong picture."

"That's funny." His voice is filled with sadness and disappointment as he shakes his head. "I thought it was the right picture. If you would have just told me that you just wanted to be friends, I would have been okay with that, Olivia."

"I know," I admit quietly, the tension hanging heavily in the air between us. "I've loved Sterling for as long as I can remember, but I always thought it wasn't a reciprocated feeling."

Noah is quiet for a moment as he just stares at me. I can't quite read the emotion that washes over his eyes, but it's not anything good. "So, you just led me on then?"

"I wasn't trying to," I tell him honestly, even though I knew that I kind of was. "I didn't want to completely count you out because we do have a connection with one another. I was curious about it and wanted to explore it, but Sterling's presence in my heart is just too loud. It's too loud for me to ignore and I couldn't let that go."

"I don't even know what to say, Olivia," he tells me, hanging his head in defeat. "I wish you would have told me this sooner. I feel like a fool and like I wasted my time. I didn't know how things would go between us, but I wish you would have at least given me the opportunity to show you how good I can be to you. Or told me so I wouldn't have continued to try to make something happen between us."

"See, that's the problem," I tell him, my voice quiet as it cracks around the words. "We shouldn't have to try to make something happen between us. It's a matter of the heart and something that should just happen organically. I think we were both just trying too hard and honestly, that would have never worked in the end."

"I understand what you're saying, but that still doesn't change how I feel about this right now," he tells me with nothing but honesty. It's not what I want to hear, but I don't have any control over what he chooses to do with his feelings. I'm the one who indirectly hurt him because I couldn't be straightforward. "I'm not saying that we can't ever be friends, but I need some time and some space from this whole situation."

I swallow hard over the lump in my throat. "I understand, Noah. And I just want you to know that I really am sorry. Especially for how Sterling acted about it."

"I'm honestly not even worried about that," he says, his eyes meeting mine again with disappointment. "Yeah, he was a dickhead about it. But it would have been a lot better coming from you instead of him. I was blindsided and I don't like how that makes me feel."

I knew I hurt him, but I didn't know he was this affected by it all. I thought Sterling saying something to him would have been the worst of it, but he's completely right and I completely understand where he's coming from. I would feel the same way. Almost like it's a betrayal of some sort.

"Just give me some time, Olivia," Noah says, his voice soft and gentle. "I don't want to lose you as a friend, but right now, this is just too close."

His words give me a sense of hope and my heart feels like it beats a little harder at the prospect. I know Sterling won't be happy about the two of us still being friends, but I'm not sure I should really care about what he says.

I don't even know where Sterling and I stand in this moment. I was the one who told him I needed some space and time to think. And I've done nothing but think about the negatives of the situation. Sterling was reacting in the way he knows how to.

That doesn't excuse it at all, but maybe I need to think about it from a different perspective. I really don't know what to do when it comes to Sterling and I'm not sure I can trust my heart in this matter.

Leaving Noah, I find my seat and sit down as everyone else begins to come into the classroom. Feeling my phone vibrating in my pocket, I pull it out, my heart in my throat as I unlock the screen. I'm not ready to talk to Sterling, but I can't help but want to hear from him. To hear his voice once again.

As I open my messages, I feel like a deflated balloon when I see that it isn't him. It's Stella instead. I haven't really talked to her, even though she's my best friend. She'd see right through me and she'd be able to tell that something is wrong. And I can't even talk to her about my problem.

STELLA

SURPRISE BITCH!!

Her message reads with a picture of her outside of Wyncote's main entrance. Another message comes through and I stare at my phone with my eyes wide.

STELLA

We're hanging out tonight. My asshole brother will pick you up after your last class. Make sure you're ready because we need to have some fun!

My stomach sinks while simultaneously rolling with dread. I reread her message again and I'm filled with the need to run—again. As far away from this damn place and my best friend's brother.

Only, I can't.

I can't outrun him and I can't outrun my problems.

It looks like I have no choice but to finally face him...

CHAPTER TWENTY-TWO
STERLING

As I pull up at campus, I can see Olivia already waiting outside for me. I knew she would be out here since Stella told her I was coming after her last class. Olivia is predictable like that, but what is unpredictable is how she's going to react to seeing me again. This is the first contact we will be having since I went and fucked everything up.

She sees me as soon as I pull up and put the car into park. Unbuckling my seat belt, I quickly get out, attempting to walk over to open the door for her, but she beats me to it. Her eyes meet mine from across the hood of the car and she narrows them at me in warning. It feels like a knife to my chest, but I suck back my pride and nod before walking back to the driver's side.

When I get back in the car, Olivia is already buckled in, staring directly out the windshield as if I don't even exist. The tension is thick between us, almost palpable, and there's an awkwardness that hangs heavily in the air. I want it to dissipate, to completely vanish, but I don't know where to even begin.

A sigh slips from my lips as I shift the car into first gear and pull away from the curb. I glance at Olivia a few times before pulling out of the parking lot, but she doesn't dare chance a glance in my direction.

"How was your day?" I ask her, my voice strangled as the words get stuck in my throat.

Olivia doesn't look at me. "Fine."

"Good," I murmur softly, turning onto a different street as we head in the direction of my house. Where my damn sister is who decided to send me on this suicide mission by myself. Luckily, she still doesn't know a thing about what's going on between Olivia and me. "I haven't seen you around lately."

"We don't have to do this, Sterling."

Her words are like a blow to the chest and it

takes me a minute to recover. "Do what?"

"Exchange pleasantries like we're friends." Her voice is flat, void of emotion as she folds her hands in her lap and turns her head to look out the window. "We were never friends and what happened between us was a mistake that never should have happened."

"You don't mean that," I tell her, the words slipping from my lips before I have a chance to stop them. "Don't say that, don't diminish what was growing between us. It wasn't a mistake."

"Maybe not for you," she scoffs, and her icy tone sends a shiver down my spine. This isn't the Olivia I've known since we were kids. The sun is gone and all that's left is a scorned, hollowed-out moon.

Words cease to exist. This is the moment where I should fight her, where I should tell her how I really feel. But I don't. I keep my lips sealed, locked tightly as I throw away the key. It wasn't a mistake, but I regret the way I fucked things up between us. She'll never forgive me and I guess it's time I accept the cold, hard truth.

Olivia Davis always looked at me like I hung the moon and the stars in the sky.

Now, she won't even look at me at all.

We ride in silence for the rest of the drive. I'm

left feeling completely defeated, like a deflated balloon as we pull up in front of my house. Olivia doesn't move as I kill the engine. She sits completely still, her gaze directed out the window as she stares absently at the house.

"I don't want to be here, Sterling," she admits, her voice crystal clear, cutting through the silence like glass. "I'm here to make your sister happy and nothing more."

I swallow hard over the knives in my throat. "Okay."

Olivia lets out a sigh as she undoes her seat belt and climbs out of the car. I'm frozen in my seat, mentally kicking myself for missing my chance. I've never been one to talk about my feelings, let alone let myself have them for someone else. Here I am, in love with my sister's best friend, and I don't even have the balls to tell her.

There's something about the vulnerability of completely letting my guard down that terrifies me. If I tell her the truth, she holds all the power. And she has the ability to completely destroy me.

Who am I kidding?

Olivia Davis already has that power...

———

When I walk into the house, Olivia and Stella are already sitting on the couch together. There's a bright smile on Olivia's face as she listens to my sister, but it doesn't quite reach her eyes and I know exactly why. Simon and Vaughn are both standing in the kitchen. Simon's gaze meets mine as I hover in the doorway.

Taking a deep breath, I walk over to him with my shoulders sagging. We both step into the kitchen, away from the girls, as he practically corners me.

"Dude, what did you do to her?"

My jaw clenches. "Nothing. I just fucked up, all right? I intervened on a friendship she had with another guy and overstepped some boundaries that I shouldn't have."

"Well, your sister has asked her like three times already if she's okay... and she's only been inside for like two minutes."

Fuck.

I need Olivia to get it together. What happened is between the two of us and the last thing I need is my goddamn sister getting involved. She can read Olivia and will be able to tell without a doubt that there's something wrong. And she won't stop until she gets to the bottom of it.

"I don't know what to do, bro," I tell Simon, my

voice quiet as I don't fully trust it. "I told myself I was going to come clean with her and tell her how I really felt, but I couldn't bring myself to do it."

"You know what you have to do, Barrett," he says, his voice stern as he grabs three beers from the fridge. He hands one to me, one to Vaughn, and keeps one for himself as he begins to head out to the living room. "Man up and fucking do it."

He's right. I need to do it... but I can't with my sister asking her a million questions.

Twisting off the cap of my bottle, I toss it onto the counter before taking a deep breath. I'm practically walking into the lion's den, but I need to go face this shit head-on. I need to make things better between Olivia and me.

Or else I need to let her go forever.

"Where are our beers?" Stella asks Simon, her bottom lip stuck out in a pout as I walk into the living room and catch him sitting down on the couch.

Simon shrugs at her. "You guys aren't underage drinking here unless your brother gives the go-ahead. He's in charge of you, not me."

Stella cocks an eyebrow at him, her lips parting like she's about to say something, but she clamps them shut as she sees me watching the two of them.

It's a weird exchange, but my sister plasters the brightest smile that she can muster as she looks up at me.

"Come on, Ster," she begs, giving me her infamous puppy dog eyes that have always gotten her, her way when we were kids. "Just one beer each?"

I look between her and Olivia, who is effectively avoiding my gaze as a sigh slips from my lips. "Fine. One beer each."

"You're the best!" Stella exclaims, clapping her hands together as she jumps to her feet. Olivia snorts, her face contorting as she rolls her eyes. Stella doesn't miss a beat, her eyebrows tugging together as she looks at Olivia in confusion.

It feels like she's twisting my heart in my chest with her reaction. I visibly wince, my jaw simultaneously clenching. My sister is looking at me now, a look of suspicion crossing her features.

"I'll get the beers," I reply gruffly.

"Good idea," Simon mumbles from where he's sitting on the couch as he flips through the channels on the TV. Vaughn is sitting near him with a look of amusement on his face.

This night is going so well... and it's just getting started.

CHAPTER TWENTY-THREE
OLIVIA

We're four beers deep when Stella pulls me into the kitchen with her. It's been awkward as hell, but the alcohol has definitely been helping me feel a little more comfortable. Although, I can't shake the way it makes me feel when Sterling looks at me. And his gaze has been practically glued to me all night long.

"Okay, Liv," Stella starts, her words slurring a little as she leans against the counter. Sterling, Simon, and Vaughn were playing some video game when Stella offered to get more beers and then dragged me along with her. Except she has me here for an interrogation. "What's going on with you and my brother?"

The air leaves my lungs in a rush and it feels like

the rug has successfully been pulled out from underneath me. My breathing falters, my heart hammering away in my chest like it's going to break free through my rib cage. "What do you mean?"

I could slap myself in the forehead for the stupid response I just gave her. The guilt is written all over my face as I stare at her with my eyes wide.

"Liv, it's cool," Stella says dismissively, drastically waving her hand at me. "I mean, it's kind of a shock, but I'll get over it. Is he the reason why you're not yourself right now?"

"I don't know what you're talking about," I tell her, shifting my weight nervously on my feet. I've never been a good liar, but I can't help but try and deny everything. It's better to ask for forgiveness than permission, right?

Stella rolls her eyes. "I love you, girl, but you're a shit liar. It's obvious. Something is going on with you and him. I'm not mad, I promise. But, tell me what that asshole did that has you upset."

"I'm fine, Stella," I answer, attempting to be dismissive, even though my voice catches in my throat. Stella doesn't miss a damn beat, her eyes narrowing as they fill with sympathy.

"You can tell me, Liv," she assures me, her voice soft and gentle as she steps toward me. She sways slightly and her hands are clammy as she wraps them around mine. "He did something to hurt you and I'm going to cut off his testicles and hand-feed them to him. But first, I want to know what he did."

I've been trying so hard to hold this all in and I can't help the tears as they begin to fall from my eyes. "I messed up, Stella. I let myself fall for him and then everything got all messed up. You remember Noah, the guy I told you about? Sterling told me I needed to get rid of him, even though we weren't dating or anything. I didn't and Sterling did."

"Ew." Stella's face scrunches up. "How fucking toxic can he be? Does he not know what boundaries are?" Her expression softens and she squeezes my hands lightly. "None of his behavior is excusable, but I'm honestly not surprised when it comes to you."

"What do you mean?"

Stella gives me a knowing look. "He's always been protective of you, Liv. Even when we were kids and you and I got into fights, he always took your side. I didn't want to put much weight on it then but as we got older, I could see how he looked at you."

My heart pounds erratically in my chest as I listen to her recount the way she's observed her brother around me. The way that she saw our relationship developing from the outside, many years ago.

"What he did was fucked up," she says, shaking her head in disappointment toward him. "He needs to learn some boundaries and how that kind of shit doesn't fly. We don't put up with that kind of toxic shit from anyone, you feel me?"

I nod. "I went with Noah to one of Sterling's games and he didn't know we were going to be there. Hell, I didn't even know until Noah picked me up. I should have just told him then that we couldn't be more than friends, but I didn't know how to. I led him on and then pissed Sterling off. And then everything just blew up in my face."

"Sterling always has had a little bit of a jealous side. And especially after a game when his emotions and adrenaline are flowing." She pauses for a moment, pursing her lips. "What he did was unacceptable, but do you feel like it was unforgivable? Like, in your eyes, is there any coming back from this?"

I stare back at her for a moment. "How are you talking to me like this, as if it's any other guy when it's your brother?"

Stella shrugs, a lopsided, drunken grin on her

face. "I'm trying to not picture the two of you in bed, okay?" She pauses, a look of disgust on her face instantly. "Oh god, I shouldn't have said it out loud because now the thought is in my mind. Okay, quick. Abort. Answer my question and distract my stupid brain."

I can't fight the soft laughter that falls from my lips. This is what I love about my best friend. She's one of my safety nets, even when it might be a difficult conversation. And she always knows how to break up the mood and make it lighter, when it has felt so damn heavy.

"No, it's not unforgivable," I tell her after running through the thoughts in my mind. "I guess I just need the assurance that it won't happen again. I won't have someone tell me who I can and can't be friends with, regardless of whether they're a guy or a girl. I'm not going to let someone else control me."

"Yes, girl, exactly!" she exclaims, releasing my hands as she claps. "You need to tell him all of this. Get him to pull his stubborn head out of his ass and come to his senses. Either that or he needs to let go of the grip he has on you so you can move on. It's a shame he went and fucked up your chances with Noah... although, he sounded as exciting as a cardboard box."

"Cardboard boxes can be fun sometimes," I retort, wincing at the mention of his name.

Stella raises an eyebrow at me. "Yeah, if you're like five years old." She takes a step away from me, her gaze filled with a look that I don't like. The look Stella gets when she's about to stir shit up. She's slowly moving her feet, inching toward the doorway that leads to where her brother is.

"Stella, don't," I tell her, my voice low with warning.

A mischievous grin tugs on the corners of her lips. They part wide and she yells for her brother and I swear to God, I want the ground to open up and swallow me whole. Sterling appears in the doorway, looking back and forth between the two of us with worry in his eyes.

"Is everything okay? Why'd you yell?"

"No, everything is not okay." Stella looks at her brother, her eyes slicing through him. "You're a goddamn idiot and you need to make things right with Olivia."

My stomach sinks and I tilt my head back to look up at the ceiling. This is not how I wanted to confront my problems, but leave it to Stella. She just had to intervene. She couldn't talk to him in private and let us hash it out. Nope. It has to be handled, right here, right now. I don't know if I blame her or the beer that she chugged more.

"I'm going to leave the two of you to it, but I don't want either of you coming out of this room until you kiss and make up."

Stella blows me a kiss and winks before she disappears through the doorway, leaving Sterling and I staring at each other from across the room. I feel completely exposed under his gaze and my lips part slightly as I release the breath I didn't realize I was holding. What the hell is supposed to happen now?

"Olivia," Sterling's voice is soft and gentle, caressing my name as he takes a step toward me. He closes the distance between us, stopping as his toes meet mine. I tilt my head back to look up at him. "I should have told you a long time ago... I'm in love with you."

CHAPTER TWENTY-FOUR
STERLING

Olivia's eyes widen as she stares up at me, her plump lips parted slightly. I should have done this earlier today when it was just the two of us and without my sister having to intervene. I can't tell what is going on in Olivia's head right now and she's staring back at me like she's in complete shock. Almost as if she's frozen in place.

"Olivia... please say something."

The silence is literally killing me. I don't need her to say it back to me. Hell, I don't know what I need to hear from her, but something is better than nothing in this moment. Right now, I can't get my heart to calm down as it pounds erratically in my chest. I've never put my heart on the line like I am in this moment.

To be honest, Olivia is the first girl I've ever had these feelings for. And the first I've ever confessed my love to. I don't care if she throws it back in my face, although that's not where I want this to go. But if that's the way she feels, then I completely understand. I can't help but feel a little relieved that I finally got it out.

"I don't know what to say, Sterling," she says, her voice a strangled whisper as she chokes over her words. Her eyes grow moist and there's a wave of pain washed over her expression, almost as if I'm hurting her. "You weren't supposed to fall in love with me."

"I know, baby. Trust me, I tried not to," I admit, reaching out to cup the side of her face as she continues to look up at me. "I couldn't fight it anymore. You consume my every thought. You worked your way into my heart and I'm afraid I can't get you out of there."

"It would never work, Sterling," she argues, shaking her head as she takes a step away from me. "You're graduating this year. You told me not to worry about what would happen in the future, but I can't do that. I have to worry about what happens in the future and if you can't give me something stable, then it's not something I feel comfortable with."

I fight the urge to follow after her, instead I allow her to create some distance between the two of us. It's almost as if it creates some sense of security for her. She's always been a flight risk and with not being cornered right now, she still has that option to exit the room in case she feels like she needs to.

Although, I hope she doesn't.

"Remember what I asked you to do that one night, Liv?"

She tilts her head to the side, her eyebrows pulling together as she shakes her head.

"I asked you to let me be one of your safety nets. I promise I won't hurt you. I will keep you safe, sunshine."

Olivia swallows roughly, her tongue slipping through her lips as she wets them. "How can I believe that, though? You're going to play hockey professionally after this. Who knows where you will even end up in the country. Hell, you could end up in Canada, for all we know."

"You're right," I agree with her, because she isn't wrong. Professional level is my next step and my future is a little unpredictable right now. "But that doesn't mean anything would have to change between us. I would never ask you to give up your degree you're working on to follow me. We could make long distance work. I will come see you every free second that I have."

I watch in confusion as two tears simultaneously fall from her eyes, streaming down the sides of her face. Through the sadness, her eyes still shine brightly at me and her lips pull upward into a sad smile. "You really believe that would work? We would be worlds apart, Sterling. I never did fit into yours."

"Don't say that, sunshine," I plead with her, my voice cracking around my words. "You are what makes my world feel like it's complete. If you don't want to be with me, I won't push you. I understand how important boundaries are and I'm trying to learn to rein myself back in when I feel jealous or possessive. But I want to be with you, Olivia. However we have to make it work, I'm willing to put in the work."

She stares back at me, but words seem to fail her in this moment. I shouldn't be springing this all on her, but she needs to know the truth, and we're progressively running out of time. The last time I saw her—the night I fucked it all up—she asked for space and time to think. I think she's had enough time.

I just need her to feel safe with me. For her to trust me with her heart because I will treat it like the most precious piece of glass. It's the one thing I would never dare to break, even if I have hurt her in the past.

"I don't think relationships are supposed to be hard," she says softly, her voice thoughtful. "Is it really worth it if we constantly have to fight to make it work?"

"Nothing good in life comes easily, sunshine... you should know this by now."

She takes a step toward me and my heart crawls into my throat. "I appreciate you being honest with me with your feelings, Sterling." Her voice is soft and gentle, but it's filled with caution. "I've been in love with you for as long as I can remember, but I don't like the thought of the risk. It scares the hell out of me."

Her words hit me with such force, it feels like my heart is about to combust. She's been in love with me for as long as she can remember. How the hell could I be so goddamn blind to it all?

"All of this scares me," I admit, a nervous chuckle rumbling in my chest. "All that I'm asking is for you to give me a chance, Olivia. I don't need an answer right now. I just wanted you to know how I feel. Whatever you decide to do with that is your choice now."

It kills me to leave the ball in her court like this, when she seems so unsure of what she wants. I believe her when she says she's been in love with me for a long time, but that doesn't change the way she feels about the future.

Walking away from her right now is one of the hardest things I've ever had to do. I can feel her eyes on my back as I turn around and walk out of the kitchen. My sister is sitting in the living room with Simon, her eyes meeting mine in question as I walk through the room. Her lips part, like she's about to say something, but I shake my head, shutting her down instantly.

I catch a glimpse of the grim look on her face that is laced with sadness. I know that Stella was only trying to help and there's a part of me that is grateful for her intrusion. She pushed me to do the one thing I had been terrified of actually doing. I wasn't expecting Olivia to fall to her knees and want to be with me, but her hesitation and fears leave me feeling unsettled.

Walking directly to the stairs, I'm halfway up

them on the way to my bedroom when I hear Olivia's voice as she speaks to my sister. She's apologizing and telling her that she wants to go home. She tells Stella they can hang out tomorrow instead after Simon offers to give her a ride home. My heart sinks and dread rolls in the pit of my stomach, but I'm not surprised. My head hangs in defeat as I make my way up to my bedroom and lock the door behind me.

Olivia feels cornered so now she's doing what she does best.

She's running.

She has always been careful—sometimes too careful that it almost hinders the way she lives her life. I don't want her to be uncomfortable and constantly worry if we're together, but I want her to take this leap with me. I want her to feel safe and to know that she's loved.

I just want her to fall with me, so I can be the one to catch her.

CHAPTER TWENTY-FIVE
OLIVIA

I don't know what to make of everything Sterling just told me. I'm partly in shock, partially elated by knowing he feels the same way about me, and absolutely terrified. Yet again, my grumpy guy is being kind and patient by giving me the time to think about it all.

My mind just doesn't even know where to begin.

There are so many variables and I hate it. I like everything planned. I like knowing what to expect. And with Sterling and the future between us, there's literally no guarantee for anything. I thought I was ready to let him break my heart, but now I'm not so sure. I don't know if it's something I would ever be able to come back from.

Simon graciously offered to give me a ride home

after Sterling disappeared upstairs. Part of me wanted to follow after him, but I really do need to think this through before I go ahead and make a rash decision. I tend to be more calculated when it comes to planning and this is definitely a big decision.

It shouldn't even be a question because of how I feel about him, but I can't help but question everything. It used to be one thing that pissed Sterling off so much, but it's like he's already making a change. He wants me to question everything and make sure I feel safe with whatever decision I decide to make.

"You know, Olivia," Simon starts as we continue down the road in the direction of Wyncote's campus. "For what it's worth, I've never seen Sterling like this with another girl. He never gets involved with anyone and he's completely captivated by you."

"I know," I say quietly. "I just can't help but worry about the future. Like what happens when he graduates and gets drafted onto a team? What happens if he moves far away and I'm still here in Vermont?"

"Do you feel the same way about him?" Simon questions me, nothing but curiosity in his voice.

A sigh slips from my lips. "I do."

"Then you do whatever you can to make it work."

Simon's words linger in my mind, swirling around as they begin to consume me. Perhaps he's right. Maybe I've been making this more complicated than it has to be. I don't know if the risk is worth the possible heartbreak, but maybe it's time I step out of my comfort zone. I need to live a little and my cautiousness has been doing nothing but holding me back.

Sterling wants to be my safety net. Would it be so bad to let him?

Simon pulls his car along the curb in front of the dorm building. He puts it in park as I unbuckle my seat belt and glance over at him.

"Thanks for the ride, Simon," I tell him graciously. "I really appreciate it."

"Of course," he smiles at me before I turn to reach for the door handle. "Just think about what you really want, Olivia. You've known Sterling long enough to know that he's a great guy. It's all scary, having feelings for someone and taking that jump, but you never know what good can come from it if you don't let yourself fall."

Climbing out of the car, I turn back to Simon, offering him a smile. "Thanks, Simon."

I close the door behind me and Simon waits by the curb until I'm safely inside my building. My mind is elsewhere as I make my way up to my room. I'm thankful when I open the door and see that the room is vacant again. As much as I'd love to be able to talk to my roommate, I'm glad to have the silence and the space to deal with my thoughts alone.

Grabbing my stuff, I head to the shower room and get a quick shower, letting the hot water cleanse my soul as I attempt to work through my thoughts. I don't know why I'm hesitating so much. It should be a no-brainer. Life is so short and if you find someone who loves you, you should let them in.

Sterling isn't a bad guy. He isn't perfect, but then again, none of us are. He messed up—we both messed up and we both acknowledged what we did and apologized. There's no sense in focusing on the past because, how can you move forward if you're hung up on things you can't change any longer?

The only thing you really have control over and can change is the present and the future. Sterling acknowledged that he overstepped boundaries—important ones that need to be in place. He has expressed that he wants to respect them, and I want to believe him. Hell, I have no reason to not believe him. But at the same time, that's taking another risky chance, hoping that someone will follow through with the changes they say they're going to make.

I don't know that I see his jealous, possessive side ever diminishing completely, but he needs to understand that he has no control over me at all. I would never do anything to intentionally hurt him or step out on him. But I want to be able to make my own decisions without feeling like I need his permission or blessing.

Unless it's something big that would affect the both of us. Then of course I would consult with him without making any decisions or doing something.

After finishing showering, I slip into a pair of comfy pajamas before climbing under the covers of my twin-sized bed. As I settle with my head against my pillow, I pull the comforter the whole way up to my chin, seeking some type of comfort. Although, it doesn't find me. Instead, I'm alone with my thoughts and I've never felt more lonely in this moment than I have before.

I shouldn't have let him walk away from me tonight. I should have followed after him. I shouldn't have left without talking to him. I don't know what I was thinking that I needed space to process my thoughts. Because all of my thoughts circle back to him and the fact that I don't think I'm ready to let go of him.

We were just getting started before things got messed up between us and it's not too late to make things right. This is our chance to do things the way we should have from the beginning. Neither of us wanted to get involved and develop these types of feelings, but it was inevitable. The universe worked against us and the magnetic pull between the two of us was something neither of us could fight.

And we both fought it out of fear.

Sterling isn't someone that I should be afraid of. I've literally trusted him my entire life and loved him for just as long. I thought it was just a simple crush when I was younger, but I was so wrong. He was my first love and I want him to be my last.

There's no sense in wasting any more time. I've already taken too much time to come to this decision when it was right in front of my face the entire time. It's just that crippling fear that consumes me sometimes. I need to stop letting it get the better of me because I'm ready to live.

I'm ready to experience life being loved by him.

————

The next day, I still haven't heard anything from Sterling and I'm grateful for the space. He told me it was my choice and he's being respectful by giving me the time to think. Stella called me this morning and begged me to go along to the boys' game, so here I am sitting in the stands with her as we watch them begin to line up for the puck drop.

"Have you talked to my brother at all?"

I shake my head at her. "I planned to tonight after the game. He wanted to give me space to think about it before deciding, but I already know what I want, Stella."

My best friend smiles over at me. "You want him."

I nod as we both turn our attention back out to the ice. Sterling, Vaughn, and Hayden are all out there playing right now. They look like a well-oiled machine with the way they move around, passing the puck back and forth to each other.

Sterling and Vaughn are both racing down on opposite sides of the ice as Hayden hangs back in the defensive zone. I watch, sitting on the edge of my seat as Sterling passes the puck to Vaughn. He's skating directly toward another goal and he moves the puck around as he's about to pass one of the defensive players on the other team.

The other player slides his skate out in an attempt to trip up Vaughn but both of their knees collide. Stella lets out an audible gasp and jumps to her feet as we watch Vaughn crumple onto the ice. The other player is down too, but he quickly climbs to his skates and gingerly skates over to the bench.

The play stops completely as Vaughn lies on the ice for a moment as Sterling and Hayden rush over to him. The entire arena falls silent and everyone is completely shocked by what just happened. Stella has her hands over her mouth and we both watch in utter shock as the boys attempt to help Vaughn onto his feet.

He's unable to put any weight on his left foot. It breaks my heart watching Sterling and Hayden practically carry him off the ice. The three of them disappear down the tunnel with the coach hot on their heels. I glance over at Stella and her face looks as white as the ice.

"That was completely fucked up," she breathes, shaking her head in disappointment. "They better call a penalty for that shit."

"I don't even know much about hockey, but that didn't look like it was something legal."

Stella frowns and her nostrils flare as she lets out a deep breath. "It wasn't at all. That was knee-to-knee contact and the player was trying to trip him. That could easily end someone's career."

"Oh no," I practically whisper. This is all new to me, so everything she's telling me is something I didn't know. "I didn't realize something like that could be so detrimental."

Stella stares at me for a moment, a mix of emotions washing over her expression. "That's the way hockey is. All it takes is one accident and your career is over. Sometimes even your life. People don't realize just how dangerous this sport is and you need to know that because of Sterling."

Tearing my eyes away from her, I look back down to the ice where they're going over the play that happened and how they're going to proceed with the penalty. I can't imagine if something were to happen to Sterling... I don't know how I would handle it.

———

Stella drops me off at my dorm after we leave the game. She spoke to her brother and got news of Vaughn's condition. He was going into surgery to try and repair his knee, but it was unlikely that he would ever play again. I can't help but feel completely devastated for all of them. The accident could have been much worse, but Vaughn's career is over. And one of Sterling's closest friends is now in the middle of surgery.

Rolling over in bed, I grab my phone from my nightstand and unlock the screen. Tapping on the messages app, I find Sterling's name and open up our thread. A smile touches my lips as I read over the last few messages between us. He was right then and it still stands true now. I can't outrun him... and I don't want to anymore.

OLIVIA

Hey... I know it's late, but are you awake?

I stare at the screen for a moment, holding in my breath. It's the middle of the night and the last thing I want to do is disturb Sterling, especially after what happened to Vaughn.

STERLING

Wide awake, actually. I just got home from the hospital.

Swallowing hard over the lump lodged in my throat, I take a deep breath before typing my response back to him. I don't know how he's going to respond, but this is my chance and I'm taking it.

OLIVIA

How is Vaughn? I was at the game with Stella and heard he was going into surgery.

I watch the three little bubbles in the corner instantly appear before his message comes through.

STERLING

His knee is completely fucked. He's in recovery now, but he's never going to fully recover. He'll never play again.

My heart sinks at the thought for Vaughn. And at the same time it terrifies me that something like that could easily happen to Sterling.

OLIVIA

Can you come over?

Sterling doesn't hesitate to respond.

STERLING

Is everything okay?

OLIVIA

Everything's fine. I just want to see
you and I don't think I can wait until
tomorrow. I want to talk to you, but
in person.

STERLING

Say no more, sunshine. I'll be there
in twenty minutes.

I reread his message a few times before locking my screen. My heart is beating to its own melody inside my chest and I hold my phone against my sternum. There's something about the way he calls me sunshine that makes my stomach flutter.

I'm ready to hand my heart over to Sterling Barrett.

Even if he decides to break it in the end.

CHAPTER TWENTY-SIX

I'm pretty positive that I break every traffic law possible as I race back to the campus. I didn't expect Olivia to text me tonight asking me to come over. I was just lying in bed, still going over the way the game unfolded and what happened to Vaughn. It's so scary the way things can happen within the blink of an eye and can literally change the course of your life.

Vaughn was destined for greatness. He had scouts looking at him since high school and there were talks of teams wanting him for the next season. All of that changed tonight from one hit. His career is officially ruined and I fucking hate that for him. It can literally happen to any of us, and to see someone with such a bright future have this happen to them really fucking sucks.

I plan on going to see him tomorrow in the hospital, but I don't know if he's going to want any visitors. I know I wouldn't. When he wakes up after surgery and finds out he's never going to play again, he's going to be devastated. Hockey is his life, so what happens when that's taken away?

As I pull into a parking spot in the lot outside of Olivia's building, I push thoughts of Vaughn and his accident from my mind. I can't focus on the negatives right now, not when I'm walking into what I hope is something good with Olivia. My entire heart is on the line right now. I handed it to her and she has the ability to completely shatter it.

The doors are locked when I walk up to the building, so I pull out my phone and find Olivia's name before pressing the call button. It rings twice before she answers.

"Hello?" she says, her voice soft, sounding like the sweetest melody my ears have ever been graced with.

"Hey," I reply quietly. "I'm outside. I think I need you to come let me in."

"Oh shoot," she says in a rush and I hear something rustling around, like she's climbing out of bed. "I didn't even think about that. I'll be right down."

"I'll be here," I assure her before ending the call. I shift my weight nervously as I stand in the cold and wait for her. I would stand in subzero temperatures for this girl, until my body was overcome with hypothermia.

Olivia wastes no time getting down to the door and she unlocks it before pushing it open for me. A rush of cold air slips in while I step inside and she shivers in her pajamas. I can't fight the grin that tugs on my lips as I see her in her fluffy pants and oversized crewneck sweatshirt.

"Hi," she says quietly, her arm brushing against mine as she locks the door again. "I'm glad you came."

I smile down at her. "I'm glad you asked me to."

She swallows hard and nods before turning around. I follow after her, taking the flight of stairs to the second floor. We walk in silence down the hall before slipping into her dorm room. Her roommate isn't here and for that, I am thankful. I'm fairly certain that Olivia wouldn't have even asked me to come here if she were home anyway.

I step into her room behind her, pushing the door shut behind me. Turning around, I switch over the lock before turning back to Olivia. She smiles at me, silently thanking me. The last thing we need is someone walking in right now. I don't know what she wants to say to me, but I don't want any interruptions. I want her all to myself right now.

Olivia walks over to her bed, sitting down before she motions for me to come over. I stride across the room, my long legs covering more ground than hers, and I stop in front of her as I reach the edge. She pats the spot on the mattress next to her and I oblige, taking a seat beside her.

She pulls her legs up onto the bed, tucking them underneath her as she grabs her pillow and holds it on her lap. It's almost as if she's guarding herself from something and I can't tell if it's from me or what she's about to unleash on me. Either way, I hate how she already has her guard up, even though she has nothing but vulnerability written across her expression.

"What did you want to talk about, sunshine?" I ask her, my voice soft and gentle to try and create a sense of security. It's not a facade. I really do want her to feel safe with me. I want her to be able to talk to me without feeling like she needs to be constantly looking for the nearest exit.

She swallows hard again and her eyes are filled

with emotion as she turns to face me. Kicking off my shoes, I pull one of my legs onto the bed, bending my knee as we sit face to face. "I wanted to talk to you about everything. You shared your truth with me and I feel like I only gave you half of mine."

I stare back at her, my eyes bouncing back and forth between hers, desperately wanting to be inside her mind right now. I'm afraid she isn't going to tell me everything and I don't want her to hold back on me. Not right now, not in this moment, and honestly, I never want her to.

"I've been in love with you for as long as I can remember, Sterling. I thought it was just a crush when we were younger and that it was something I would be able to get over, but I never could. Regardless of how badly I tried, I could never get you out of my mind. I was constantly comparing everyone else to you and no one could ever live up to you."

Emotion wells in my throat and I reach out, my hand gentle as my fingertips stroke the soft skin on the side of her face. She stares back at me and I swear I could get lost in the depths of her irises and never surface again.

"I'm not going to lie to you and tell you I'm not terrified. You know how I am. I don't do anything without thinking it through to the tiniest details possible. But there was something you told me that has stuck with me since. I haven't truly been living life with how reserved I am about everything. I keep my guard up and don't let people in because of the fear of getting hurt. Hell, I'm literally afraid of every- thing, which is why I do everything so cautiously and carefully."

"I know, sunshine," I tell her, cupping the side of her face as I slowly drag my thumb across her cheek. Her eyelids flutter shut and she leans against me, a sigh slipping from her lips. "You're safe with me, Olivia. I can always promise you that. I would never do anything to hurt you, ever."

"That's what really scares me, but you know what I realized? Even if I do get hurt in the end, I would be missing out by not experiencing life being loved by you."

Her words have my breath catching in my throat. I stare back at her, emotion flooding my body as I feel tears prick the corners of my eyes. I've never been one to let myself feel this deeply or to cry, but there's something about the way she's being with me right now that has me completely consumed by my feelings.

"I want to be with you, Sterling. I don't care about the details and what happens in the future. I love you and you are the only person I have ever wanted." She pauses for a moment, a smile pulling on the corners of her lips. "Whatever happens, we will always make it work. We can figure it all out as we come across different obstacles. I'm ready to fall... I just have one question for you."

I stare back at her. "Ask me, baby."

"Will you be the one to catch me?"

I'm literally choked up and my vision blurs with the tears that now fill my eyes. "I will always be the one to catch you and I will never fucking drop you. I swear on my life, I will never let you go, sunshine. You're the sun that shines from my skies, even on the darkest days. You're the only thing I want as a constant in my life."

"Well, except hockey." She laughs lightly and the sound caresses my eardrums like the softest silk.

"Hockey doesn't come close to touching how important you are to me," I tell her with nothing but honesty. "Yeah, it's my passion and what I want to make a career out of, but you're who I want a life with."

A smile consumes her face and tears begin to fall from her eyes. Scooting closer to her, I cup both sides of her face, catching them with my thumbs as they slide down her cheeks. "I love you, Olivia Davis. So fucking much."

"I love you too, Sterling," she breathes as she stares directly into my soul.

Pulling her closer to me, our mouths collide and I'm lost in the moment with her. I want to be lost in every moment with her for the rest of my life. We have so much time ahead of us, so much to work out, but I know we can make this work.

Our love is something that has been building for many years.

And I'm ready to let it sweep us away.

EPILOGUE
STERLING

SIX MONTHS LATER

Standing in front of the door to our hotel room, I'm a fucking goner as I stare at my beautiful wife standing in front of me. She's absolutely breathtaking with her long hair hanging in soft curls that frame her face. Her white lace dress hugs her body in all the right places. She looks as amazing as she did when I watched her walk down the aisle to me in front of all our friends and family a few hours earlier.

Everything had happened so fast between the two of us, but neither of us could wait after we were officially in a relationship together. I literally only waited two months before proposing to her. My heart and soul knew she was it for me and I wasn't about to waste any more time. I needed her to be mine and she didn't want to wait any longer either.

After we got engaged, I was drafted into the NHL. The team that drafted me was in New York, so it wasn't too far away. It wouldn't make it hard for us to travel back and forth. We decided that we wanted to get married before the summer was over, so we made our plans as quickly as possible and we were married here in Vermont under the summer sun.

A smile tugs on the corners of my lips as I stalk over to my beautiful bride. She lets out a yelp as I scoop her up into my arms and carry her into our hotel room. Kicking the door shut behind us, Olivia laughs as I carry her straight to the bed and lay her down on the plush mattress. I follow after her, climbing over her as I hover above her body.

"You're the most beautiful woman I'll ever see, Mrs. Barrett."

Olivia smiles up at me. "You're not so bad yourself, Mr. Barrett."

I want to rip her dress off of her, tearing the lace material into a million shredded pieces as I throw them onto the floor. She's already told me a million times how much she loves this dress, so I won't do that to her. But fuck, I need her naked and underneath me right now.

Pushing myself away from her and off the bed, I tower above her for a moment as Olivia sits up. Leaning forward, I grab her hands and pull her to her feet with me. She instinctively wraps her arms around the back of my neck, her bright eyes meeting mine with a smile in them.

"I can't believe you're finally my wife," I murmur, my mouth dipping down to hers. "This is real life."

"It is," Olivia breathes against my lips. "And this is forever, baby."

Capturing her mouth with my own, I steal the air from her lungs. She kisses me back, her lips soft and warm against mine. She tastes like the champagne we drank at our toast at the end of the wedding and my tongue slides against hers, tasting the bubbly flavor.

Breaking apart, I grip her hips and spin her around to face the bed. My hands lift to her shoulders, feeling her soft skin under my palms. Dipping forward, I press my lips against her neck, kissing my way across her shoulders as my hands drop down to the zipper of her dress. Pulling on it, I slide the zipper until it meets resistance, just above her ass.

Without any straps, it easily falls away from her body, pooling on the floor around her feet. I slide my hands up along her spine, unclasping her bra as I reach it. Grabbing the material in my hand, I toss it onto the floor. Olivia is standing in front of me, facing away with nothing on but a thong and her heels.

I take a step back, my hands undoing the tie from my neck, and Olivia turns around to face me as I drop it onto the floor. She lifts her feet, stepping away from her dress as she inches closer to me. Her touch is gentle as she reaches for my suit jacket and pushes it away from my shoulders. I let it slide down my arms before it lands on the floor with the rest of our clothing.

Olivia is quick as she slides each button from my dress shirt through the holes. The urgency builds within me and as she nears the bottom of my shirt, I grab the material from her and pull on it. It tears the remaining few buttons from their threads, popping and flying across the room as I rip the rest of my shirt off. Her eyes find mine in a rush and a bubbly laugh falls from her lips.

Tossing it to the floor, my hands find her hips and I back her up to the bed, lightly pushing her down onto it. A gasp escapes her and she's breathless, her cheeks tinted pink as she stares up at me from where she's now laying. My hands find the buckle of my belt and it takes me about two seconds to remove the rest of my clothes from my body.

Stepping closer to the bed, I drop down onto my knees, grabbing Olivia's hips as I drag her closer to me. She lets out a yelp, her head lifting up off the bed as her wild eyes find mine. A smile tugs on the corners of my lips as I slide my fingers underneath the straps of her thong before pulling them down. I strip off her underwear before it finds its way with the rest of our clothing.

"My shoes," Olivia mumbles as she starts to lift herself from the bed. I plant my palm against her stomach, effectively pushing her down.

"Leave them," I murmur, grabbing her thighs as I hook her knees over my shoulders. Planting my lips against her soft skin, I suck and taste my way to the apex of her legs. A sigh escapes her as I drag my tongue along her center, tasting that sweet pussy.

"Mmm," I murmur against her flesh, sucking her clit between my lips. "My wife tastes fucking amazing."

Olivia's hands slide into my hair. "And I want my husband to make me come."

"Say no more, sunshine," I smile against her

before I devour her. Sliding my tongue along her, I lap at her pussy, each time circling around her clit. Her fingers grip my hair tighter, holding my head in place as her hips buck against my face. Suctioning my lips around her clit, I roll the bundle of nerves around with my tongue, driving her closer and closer to the edge.

"Oh god, Sterling," Olivia moans loudly as I continue to work her clit with my tongue. "I'm so close."

"Come for me, baby," I murmur against her pussy. "Let me taste you on my tongue."

She moans again as I dive back in, not coming up for air as I lose myself in her pleasure. I work my mouth against her, fucking her with it until she's screaming out my name, shattering into a million fucking pieces. Her legs clamp around my head, her body shaking as her orgasm tears through her body.

I lick and suck her flesh as she rides the wave of her high, lapping up every last drop from my wife. I still can't get over it. She's my fucking wife and I get to spend the rest of my life doing this with her. Lifting my head away from her, Olivia is breathless, her chest heaving with every breath as I climb onto the bed with her.

Rolling her onto her side, I lie behind her as the

big spoon. She lifts her one leg, reaching between us as she grabs my cock and guides me inside her. Shifting my hips, I thrust into her, filling her to the brim. She's soaking wet with her arousal and goddamn, she feels fucking amazing.

Spooning her, I rock my hips, slowly fucking her as I slide one arm under her neck and pull her back flush against my front. My other hand finds her stomach and I lightly trace patterns across her skin.

"I want to put a baby inside you, sunshine. I want to see your stomach swollen and round as our baby grows inside of you."

Her breath catches in her throat. "Is that really what you want?"

"Fuck yes, it is. That's all I want with you. And as soon as you have that baby, I'm going to put another one in you."

Olivia laughs lightly. "That's going to be a lot of kids."

"I want as many as you'll give me."

I slide my cock in and out of her, the moans falling from her lips as I slide my hand up to her breasts. Cupping one in my hand, I roll her nipple with my fingers, pinching and pulling on her flesh as I continue to fuck her. Each thrust grows more urgent and Olivia pushes her ass against me, arching her back.

Unable to hold back anymore, I abandon her tit and slide my hand down to grip her hip. I begin to pound into her from behind, both of us moving together on the bed as we get lost in the state of ecstasy together. It isn't long before her pussy is clenching around me and she's shattering, coming around my cock.

I pound into her once more as my balls constrict, drawing closer to my body, and the explosion hits me at full force. I lose myself deep inside her, filling her with my cum as we both fall into the great abyss of euphoria together. My thrusts become slower until I fall still. Wrapping my arms around her, I pull my wife to my chest and hold her as we attempt to catch our breaths.

"Sterling, I have something I want to tell you."

"What is it, sunshine?"

She's quiet for a second, turning her head to look at me over her shoulder. "I'm transferring schools to New York. I've already got everything in motion and I'm good to start there in the fall."

I stare at her for a moment, completely taken by shock. "Wait, what? You're moving to New York with me? I can't ask you to give up Wyncote's program for me."

Olivia smiles. "You didn't. I want to do this. It's you and me forever, baby."

"You and me forever." I smile back at her, burying my face in the crook of her neck.

We have a long way to go, but we're in this together.

And nothing can come between our love.

———

Want more of Sterling and Olivia?
Click here for an exclusive bonus scene!!

———

Coast to Coast is the seventh book from the Wyncote Wolves, featuring Simon and Stella. Continue reading below for a look inside Coast to Coast

PROLOGUE

Stella

· · ·

Sitting on the couch, I glance over at Simon whose eyes are glued to mine. A smirk tugs on the corner of his mouth and he remains silent as he raises a finger to his lips. My brother, Sterling, is arguing with his girlfriend, Olivia, about the movie that we just watched. I let out a yawn, lifting my arms up as I stretch out my spine.

My eyes glance back and forth between the two of them as they both rise to their feet. I'm not even paying attention to their futile argument anymore. It's still kind of weird, seeing my brother and my best friend in a relationship, but honestly, I don't think that there is anyone better for either of them.

"Look," I start as I grab one of the blankets draped over the back of the couch and pull it down onto my lap. "I'm pretty damn tired and you guys are in my bedroom right now. Care to take this somewhere else?"

Simon coughs to cover up his laugh as Sterling and Olivia both turn to look at me. Sterling narrows his eyes, giving me his infamous dirty look, while Olivia smiles at me.

"I'm so sorry, Stell," she says, her voice soft and gentle as she slides her hand into Sterling's. "We'll go upstairs so you can get some sleep. And maybe then your brother will come to his senses and agree with me."

"Doubtful," Sterling grumbles, shaking his head as he follows after Olivia. "The ending was done artfully. It leaves it open to each viewer's interpretation."

"No way," Olivia scoffs, rolling her eyes at him. "There needed to be more closure."

The two of them disappear upstairs and a sigh slips from my lips as I unfold the blanket and lay it across my body. Grabbing one of the pillows that they gave me to use, I tuck it in the corner of the sectional couch and flop down, pulling the blanket with me. Lifting my head, I glance over at Simon, who is sitting there with an eyebrow cocked.

"You want me to leave?" he questions me, his voice hoarse as his steel gray eyes search mine.

I swallow roughly and shake my head. "You can stay, as long as you're quiet."

"And what if I'm not?"

"Then you can go to your room too," I tell him. "Believe it or not, it's exhausting sleeping on a couch every night."

Simon stares at me for a moment and I'm lost in the metallic color of his eyes. "You can take my bed and I'll sleep down here."

A soft laugh escapes me and I shake my head at him. "I appreciate the offer, but I only have a few more days here, so it's not that big of a deal. I'm ready to head back to California, though."

Simon's eyebrows pull together slightly. "You grew up on the East Coast, right? What's so special about the west?"

"Nothing special," I reply with a shrug, attempting to get more comfortable on the couch. "It's just a lot different there. Nothing seems to slow down whereas it almost feels like we move on island time here. And it's much warmer."

"Yuck." Simon's face contorts. "How are you supposed to play lake hockey then?"

Rolling my eyes, I shake my head at him as another laugh escapes me. "Such a one-track mind... you skate indoors, like normal people."

"That's boring."

I raise an eyebrow at him, the corners of my lips twitching. "You're boring."

Simon's tongue darts out as he wets his lips and my gaze is instantly drawn to the act. "I'm far from boring, baby. You want me to show you?"

"Nice try, Simon, but I'm not falling for that one."

He simply shrugs as he rises to his feet. My eyes

widen as he begins to move over to me. He stops beside the couch, hovering above me. Rolling onto my back, our gazes collide and my breath catches in my throat. The way his dark hair hangs in waves down to his ears is distracting me.

He's been my brother's roommate for the past four years. I'm not blind, so of course I've noticed him every damn time I've been here. That doesn't change anything. The furthest we've ever gone was flirting and I can't let it go past that. As fun as it would be, I have an entire life in California... which includes a boyfriend.

"What are you doing, Simon?" I whisper as he bends down, caging me in with his hands on either side of my head.

He tilts his head to the side, his steel eyes burning holes through mine. There's a look of mischief in his gaze that melts with something indistinguishable. Suddenly, he pulls the pillow out from under my head. My head lifts up before falling back onto the couch in a rush.

Simon stands back up, clutching the pillow as a soft chuckle vibrates in his chest. My face contorts, my eyes slicing to his.

"What the hell was that for?"

He tosses the pillow onto the other side of the

sectional as his lips lift into a grin "That's my pillow and you're in my spot."

My eyebrows tug together as I abruptly sit up. "What are you talking about? I've been sleeping here the past week, using that pillow that my brother gave me to use."

Simon shakes his head at me. "You're sleeping in my bed until you leave. I'll take the couch."

"No thanks," I shake my head, attempting to stay strong against his persistence. "I'm not sleeping between your dirty-ass sheets that you've had other girls in."

Simon raises an eyebrow at me. "Are you jealous, Stella?"

"Absolutely not," I lie through my teeth, cringing. "I have a boyfriend, just so you know."

Simon snorts. "Like that really means anything."

I stare back at him in disbelief. The audacity of this asshole. I don't know if I should be more offended that he thinks I would cheat on my boyfriend or if I should be pissed off at his cockiness. Like he can get any girl he wants. Ignoring Simon, I rise to my feet, abandoning my spot on the couch as I walk around the back of it.

"Where are you going?"

I glance at him as I pause in the doorway. "To get some sleep since you won't leave me alone."

The corners of Simon's lips lift. "Ah, so you can follow directions."

I scoff, rolling my eyes before turning my back to him as I begin to exit the room.

"Stella," I hear his voice call out from where he's now laying on the couch. Turning around, I look back at him again with slight irritation written across my expression. "For the record, my sheets are clean. No other girl has ever been in my bed."

My breath catches in my throat as his steel gray eyes burn holes through mine from across the room. My heart pounds erratically in my chest, my lips parting, but words fail me. Instead, I simply nod before spinning on my heel and hightailing it out of the living room.

God forbid I stick around here any longer.

I might do something stupid... like ask him to join me in his bed.

Click HERE to continue reading Coast to Coast!!

STERLING AND OLIVIA
BONUS SCENE

The adjustment to moving to New York wasn't easy on Olivia or myself. We both moved at least two hundred miles away from everyone we knew. Olivia was in her sophomore year at a new school, Seabring University, and I was in my rookie year playing for the Brooklyn Bobcats.

My schedule has been demanding as hell and by the end of the day, I'm literally exhausted. Olivia never seems to mind. Even when I fall asleep on the couch almost every single evening, she's right there by my side. I owe a lot to her and her support. I didn't ask her to leave everything in her life to be with me, but a piece of me would definitely be missing if she weren't here.

After a grueling practice, I'm deadass tired as I

take off my gear in the locker room. A lot of the guys have been welcoming, but it's different here. I'm the new guy and my skill level is nowhere near the seasoned players'. I may have been good in college, but playing professionally is a whole different game now.

"What are you doing tonight, Barrett?" one of the other rookies, Quinn, questions me as I'm slipping my feet into my sneakers. "Some of the guys were going to go get some beers, if you wanted to come along."

I shake my head, glancing at my phone before tucking it in my pocket. A smile touches my lips. My lock screen is a picture from our wedding. A day that I'll never fucking forget.

"I appreciate the offer, but I have something better than beers waiting for me at home."

Quinn cocks an eyebrow. "That hot little wife of yours?"

I narrow my eyes at him. "Watch it."

"Hey, I don't blame you," he chuckles, throwing his hands up defensively. "If I had that to go home to, I'd be saying fuck these guys too."

Quinn offers me a smile and a wink before he disappears over with some of our other teammates. I can't help but feel a little sad for him as I watch the group of single guys head out. I was in that position once, except I thought that being alone was what I wanted. Quinn, on the other hand, seems like he wishes he had someone to go home to.

Pushing those thoughts from my mind, I head out of the building without a second glance. All of this will still be here when I come back tomorrow, but right now, all I care about is getting home to my girl. It doesn't matter how exhausted I am and that my body just wants to crawl into bed and pass out. All that really matters to me is seeing Olivia.

By the time I get home, it's already dark outside. Every light is on inside our small Cape Cod style home. A smile touches my lips as I pull into the driveway and climb out of the car. Olivia always waits for me like this every night. My feet can't carry me quick enough to the front door and I find it unlocked as I turn the knob and push it open.

"I'm home, sunshine!" I call out to her, the excitement in my voice a contradiction to the exhaustion that fills my body. The house is weirdly silent and I hear no response from Olivia as I close the door behind me and walk into the foyer.

The aroma of dinner drifts from the kitchen and I think that maybe she's in there cooking. When I step into the room, I see that she's nowhere to be found. There's food in pots on the stove, the temperature set low to keep them warm, but still no Olivia.

I can't help the panic that sets in as I glance over to the dining area. The table is set and there isn't a single thing that is out of place. Dread rolls in the pit of my stomach. Where is she?

"Olivia!" I yell out her name, the panic laced within my tone. "Where are you?"

Still nothing. I'm met with silence and my legs begin to move before my brain has time to process. My feet pound heavily against the hardwood floors as I search the first floor for her. I'm out of breath, my heart pounding erratically in my chest, and I feel like I could vomit at the same time.

"Olivia, baby," I practically plead, raising my voice as I begin to run upstairs.

"I'm up here," I hear her voice, distant as it comes from our bedroom. A sigh of relief slips from my lips and I feel like I can breathe again. "I'm in the bedroom."

"Jesus Christ," I exhale loudly as I walk into the bedroom and see her standing on the far side. "You scared the shit out of me. I started to panic when you didn't answer and I couldn't find you anywhere."

"I'm sorry to scare you," she says, her voice soft

and gentle. Ever so slowly, she turns around to face me with tears streaming down the sides of her face. "I have something I need to tell you."

Worry instantly floods me and I close the distance between us as I meet her by the window. Grabbing the sides of her face, I stare down at her, my eyes desperately searching hers. "What's wrong, sunshine? What's going on?"

Olivia lifts a small plastic stick in between us, showing me two bright lines on a screen that you couldn't possibly miss. "I'm pregnant."

The air leaves my lungs in a rush. My eyes widen as I search hers and my heart feels like it could beat its way out of my chest. "What?" I breathe, my voice catching in my throat.

"I'm so sorry, Sterling," Olivia begins to cry, the tears falling rapidly down the sides of her face. "I know this isn't the best time to have a baby and I'm just sorry. When I didn't get my period last week, I thought maybe it was just late... but then it never came. So, I went and bought a test this morning and finally brought myself to taking it before you got here."

I stare at her in shock, feeling my heart growing in my chest as an elated feeling fills me. A soft chuckle rumbles in my chest and I swipe the tears away from her face as a grin consumes my lips. "Baby, don't you dare apologize. There's never a perfect time to have a baby. This is amazing and probably the best thing you could have told me."

Dropping down to my knees, I stare at her flat stomach as I lift up her shirt. Olivia stares down at me, watching me as I press my lips to her soft skin. "There's a little person growing in here, sunshine." I pause, looking up at her as I rest my chin against her. "*Our* little person."

Olivia cups the sides of my face, staring down at me with her eyes damp. "You mean you're not upset by this at all?"

A chuckle slips from my lips and I shake my head. "What do you think I've been trying to do this whole time?"

The lilt of Olivia's laugh slides across my eardrums and she's pulling me to my feet. I stand up beside her, looking down at my beautiful wife.

My beautiful *pregnant* wife.

"I love you, Olivia. With every piece of my goddamn soul. I'm beyond ready for this chapter in life with you. I know it won't be easy, but I don't fucking care about any of that. We will always make it work and this will be amazing."

Olivia stares up at me, tears filling her eyes

again. "I love you, Sterling. How do you always know the right things to say?"

"It's just part of my charm, sunshine." I laugh lightly, pulling her against me as I wrap my arms around her waist. "Don't forget, you're the one who married me."

Olivia looks up at me, a smile stretching across her lips. "You're damn right I did."

NEXT IN THE SERIES

Coast to Coast is the seventh book from the Wyncote Wolves, featuring Simon and Stella. Continue reading on the next page for a look inside Coast to Coast.

PROLOGUE
STELLA

Sitting on the couch, I glance over at Simon whose eyes are glued to mine. A smirk tugs on the corner of his mouth and he remains silent as he raises a finger to his lips. My brother, Sterling, is arguing with his girlfriend, Olivia, about the movie that we just watched. I let out a yawn, lifting my arms up as I stretch out my spine.

My eyes glance back and forth between the two of them as they both rise to their feet. I'm not even paying attention to their futile argument anymore. It's still kind of weird, seeing my brother and my best friend in a relationship, but honestly, I don't think that there is anyone better for either of them.

"Look," I start as I grab one of the blankets draped over the back of the couch and pull it down onto my lap. "I'm pretty damn tired and you guys are in my bedroom right now. Care to take this somewhere else?"

Simon coughs to cover up his laugh as Sterling and Olivia both turn to look at me. Sterling narrows his eyes, giving me his infamous dirty look, while Olivia smiles at me.

"I'm so sorry, Stell," she says, her voice soft and gentle as she slides her hand into Sterling's. "We'll go upstairs so you can get some sleep. And maybe then your brother will come to his senses and agree with me."

"Doubtful," Sterling grumbles, shaking his head as he follows after Olivia. "The ending was done artfully. It leaves it open to each viewer's interpretation."

"No way," Olivia scoffs, rolling her eyes at him. "There needed to be more closure."

The two of them disappear upstairs and a sigh slips from my lips as I unfold the blanket and lay it across my body. Grabbing one of the pillows that they gave me to use, I tuck it in the corner of the sectional couch and flop down, pulling the blanket with me. Lifting my head, I glance over at Simon, who is sitting there with an eyebrow cocked.

"You want me to leave?" he questions me, his voice hoarse as his steel gray eyes search mine.

I swallow roughly and shake my head. "You can stay, as long as you're quiet."

"And what if I'm not?"

"Then you can go to your room too," I tell him. "Believe it or not, it's exhausting sleeping on a couch every night."

Simon stares at me for a moment and I'm lost in the metallic color of his eyes. "You can take my bed and I'll sleep down here."

A soft laugh escapes me and I shake my head at him. "I appreciate the offer, but I only have a few more days here, so it's not that big of a deal. I'm ready to head back to California, though."

Simon's eyebrows pull together slightly. "You grew up on the East Coast, right? What's so special about the west?"

"Nothing special," I reply with a shrug, attempting to get more comfortable on the couch. "It's just a lot different there. Nothing seems to slow down whereas it almost feels like we move on island time here. And it's much warmer."

"Yuck." Simon's face contorts. "How are you supposed to play lake hockey then?"

Rolling my eyes, I shake my head at him as

another laugh escapes me. "Such a one-track mind... you skate indoors, like normal people."

"That's boring."

I raise an eyebrow at him, the corners of my lips twitching. "You're boring."

Simon's tongue darts out as he wets his lips and my gaze is instantly drawn to the act. "I'm far from boring, baby. You want me to show you?"

"Nice try, Simon, but I'm not falling for that one."

He simply shrugs as he rises to his feet. My eyes widen as he begins to move over to me. He stops beside the couch, hovering above me. Rolling onto my back, our gazes collide and my breath catches in my throat. The way his dark hair hangs in waves down to his ears is distracting me.

He's been my brother's roommate for the past four years. I'm not blind, so of course I've noticed him every damn time I've been here. That doesn't change anything. The furthest we've ever gone was flirting and I can't let it go past that. As fun as it would be, I have an entire life in California... which includes a boyfriend.

"What are you doing, Simon?" I whisper as he bends down, caging me in with his hands on either side of my head.

He tilts his head to the side, his steel eyes burning holes through mine. There's a look of mischief in his gaze that melts with something indistinguishable. Suddenly, he pulls the pillow out from under my head. My head lifts up before falling back onto the couch in a rush.

Simon stands back up, clutching the pillow as a soft chuckle vibrates in his chest. My face contorts, my eyes slicing to his.

"What the hell was that for?"

He tosses the pillow onto the other side of the sectional as his lips lift into a grin "That's my pillow and you're in my spot."

My eyebrows tug together as I abruptly sit up. "What are you talking about? I've been sleeping here the past week, using that pillow that my brother gave me to use."

Simon shakes his head at me. "You're sleeping in my bed until you leave. I'll take the couch."

"No thanks," I shake my head, attempting to stay strong against his persistence. "I'm not sleeping between your dirty-ass sheets that you've had other girls in."

Simon raises an eyebrow at me. "Are you jealous, Stella?"

"Absolutely not," I lie through my teeth, cringing. "I have a boyfriend, just so you know."

Simon snorts. "Like that really means anything."

I stare back at him in disbelief. The audacity of this asshole. I don't know if I should be more offended that he thinks I would cheat on my boyfriend or if I should be pissed off at his cockiness. Like he can get any girl he wants. Ignoring Simon, I rise to my feet, abandoning my spot on the couch as I walk around the back of it.

"Where are you going?"

I glance at him as I pause in the doorway. "To get some sleep since you won't leave me alone."

The corners of Simon's lips lift. "Ah, so you can follow directions."

I scoff, rolling my eyes before turning my back to him as I begin to exit the room.

"Stella," I hear his voice call out from where he's now laying on the couch. Turning around, I look back at him again with slight irritation written across my expression. "For the record, my sheets are clean. No other girl has ever been in my bed."

My breath catches in my throat as his steel gray eyes burn holes through mine from across the room. My heart pounds erratically in my chest, my lips parting, but words fail me. Instead, I simply nod before spinning on my heel and hightailing it out of the living room.

God forbid I stick around here any longer.

I might do something stupid... like ask him to join me in his bed.

ALSO BY CALI MELLE

<u>**WYNCOTE WOLVES SERIES**</u>

Cross Checked Hearts

Deflected Hearts

Playing Offsides

The Faceoff

The Goalie Who Stole Christmas

Splintered Ice

Coast to Coast

Off-Ice Collision

ABOUT THE AUTHOR

Cali Melle is a contemporary romance author who loves writing stories that will pull at your heart-strings. You can always expect her stories to come fully equipped with heartthrobs and a happy ending, along with some steamy scenes and some sports action. In her free time, Cali can usually be found spending time with her family or with her nose in a book. As a hockey and figure skating mom, you can probably find her freezing at a rink while watching her kids chase their dreams.